Forget me Not

The Wildest Dream

Kirsty White

SCHOLASTIC

Scholastic Children's Books
Commonwealth House, 1–19 New Oxford Street,
London WC1A 1NU, UK
A division of Scholastic Ltd
London ~ New York ~ Toronto ~ Sydney ~ Auckland

First published by Scholastic Ltd, 1998

Copyright © Kirsty White, 1998

ISBN 0 590 13941 X

Typeset by TW Typesetting, Midsomer Norton Somerset
Printed and bound by Cox & Wyman Ltd, Reading, Berks

10 9 8 7 6 5 4 3 2 1

Chapter 1

Elizabeth gazed out of the window. A soft rain was falling, and mist was drifting lazily in the hollows of the park around the castle. She had breakfasted alone and the day before her was empty. She never thought that she would miss her sister Sarah, with her vanity and her high, affected laugh, but she did. Sarah was married now to the eldest son and heir of Lord Homerton; she would be settling in to her home on the estate in Sussex, far away across the sea in England. Sarah had said that she was glad to leave Ireland, with its mists and its music, the wild, wild land untamed by anyone. It was a heathen place, she said, the castle with its lands that stretched as far as the eye could see, so far that the nearest neighbours were a half day's drive away, Dublin a day more than that.

The castle was old, the tower and great hall as old as time itself, Elizabeth thought, though an ancestral Roscawl had built on two wings a hundred years before, adding graceful Georgian rooms and corridors to the ancient Celtic stone.

Sarah did not count the village in her calculations. Unlike Elizabeth, she had never played hide-and-seek with the village children in the meadow beyond the park, or roared as the boys played makeshift shinty with windfall wood and a cock made out of a pine cone.

It was not done for a daughter of the castle to know the village children. The villagers, tenants of her father, Catholic, Irish speaking and poor, were a breed apart. The rules of society dictated that there should be no contact between the village and the castle beyond the payment of rent. Elizabeth never did understand why and nor did she understand why the villagers had to pay rent. It seemed unfair that the poor should have to pay the rich when common sense would have it the other way round. She asked her brother Albert about it once, but Albert just smiled at her in that way of his that said that she did not understand because she was female and younger than him, but she would, in time, when she grew up.

Elizabeth was grown up now, to all intents and purposes. At sixteen, she was considered old enough to take her place in society, to begin the search for a suitable husband, though the thought of marriage to a man like Johnny Homerton appalled her. But she still did not understand and she thought that she never would. The villagers were not to blame for being poor, just as she was not to blame for being rich; it was an accident of birth, that was all. She could just as well be one of them as who she was.

It had been years since she had seen the village children, since her father had seen her talking to them one day and told her mother, who had asked her what she was doing and then, when Elizabeth did not immediately answer, reminded her sharply that she was the daughter of a lord, that it was not her place to have anything to do with the villagers. After that, her governess had watched her carefully and she could not slip away; and even if she could have done, she was afraid to in case someone else saw her and the village children got into trouble for being friendly with her.

Then, last year, when her governess left, Sarah had been betrothed and had drawn her into the frantic rounds of jollifications that had ended with her wedding to Johnny Homerton last week. There had been no time to go and see the village children because Sarah always had something to do – a new gown to try, or a list of invitations to write or thank-you letters to send. At eighteen, Sarah was only two years older than her, but it felt like a lifetime.

Elizabeth sighed, turned away from the window and studied herself in the silver mirror set on top of her dressing-table. Her fair hair framed her face, her dress, of soft blue velvet, was the same shade as her eyes. She had grown a lot recently, her breasts strained at the bodice of the dress which was cut demurely, like a girl's. Her mother had said something about sending to London for cloth, getting a seamstress to come and make Elizabeth new gowns because it was time she had a decent wardrobe, now that she was ready to take her place in society. Elizabeth wondered why she couldn't just get the woman from Cork to come, or maybe someone from Dublin – that would be cheaper and just as good, but her mother wouldn't hear of it. Like Sarah she thought of all things Irish as primitive and pagan, good enough only for children or the barefoot village peasants who worked on the land. Vaguely, Elizabeth had heard her father saying something about the damned repeal being the ruin of them all; she had taken that to mean that the estate was not making much money, but when she had asked about it her mother said it was just stuff and politics, nothing at all to worry about.

She rang a bell, waited for a moment and then asked Eithne, her maid, to get out her riding coat and skirt and boots, and to tell the stable-lad to saddle up her pony.

There was nothing to do indoors, and a milky sun was melting the mist. Her father was in London, her mother resting after the excitement of the wedding; there was nobody to watch over her any more.

Michael was the nicest of the village children, the one who had spoken to her when she met them so many years ago, when she was first allowed to ride her pony around the grounds alone and she had heard the screams of laughter coming from the weeping willow that draped its branches around the meadow where the sheep grazed sometimes, in the spring, with their newborn lambs.

He came over to her, asked her what her name was and then told her his and the other children's, pointing them out one by one as they hid, shyly, in the leaves. She did not remember all the names at first, but she never forgot his, nor the way that he said she could play with them, if she stuck to the rules of the game and didn't expect any special privileges because she was the daughter of Lord Roscawl.

It was the first time Elizabeth had ever played, beyond the sedate nursery games she shared with Sarah under the watchful eye of her governess, and she had never known the joy of running free and chasing, hiding and being caught. After she met the village children, she used to slip away to play with them each day in the summer, when the morning lessons were over and Sarah was having her afternoon nap. Nobody from the castle knew. It was her secret, the one she shared with Michael.

Michael was a great one for stories, tales of witches and warlocks and leprechauns, and the warriors who used to rule the land in the old days, before the English came. He told her that Ireland had kings as well, who had fled when Henry sent his armies over. Elizabeth had always thought of herself as Irish, but Michael said she was really English, because the first Roscawl was an English army officer who had won the land in a fight with the Irish three hundred years ago. It didn't matter that her family had lived here ever since. "I want to be Irish," she had said once. He laughed and told her that she did not, because to be Irish was to live in a tiny cottage and work a few acres, grow barely enough to live on once the rent was paid, to own only a cow and one set of ragged clothes; unlike the dozens of gowns that Elizabeth had, the horses in the stables and the food that appeared as if by magic three times a day.

But Michael and the other children laughed and had fun, whilst the castle was a sombre place of long, echoing corridors and muted voices. Her family rarely laughed and never seemed to have any fun; entertainment was stilted conversation, the children speaking only when spoken to, or her mother playing the piano as Sarah sang in a sharp, high-pitched voice that was slightly off-key.

There had not been much affection in Elizabeth's life; the only true tenderness that she had known had come from Nanny O'Dwyer, the Irish woman who had cared for her when she was young. When she was upset after Michael said that she was not Irish, she had gone to Nanny O'Dwyer and Nanny O'Dwyer assured her that Irish blood did run in her veins, after all. She would not explain at the time, she said that she would tell her all about it later. The sad thing was that Nanny O'Dwyer had died not long after that; she never had time to tell Elizabeth anything else. It still hurt to think about her death; Elizabeth had loved her in a way that she did not love anyone else.

Michael told her once that his family lived on potatoes, all year long, with a little soda bread for a treat on Sunday maybe, a rasher of bacon once in a blue moon. The potatoes grew closely together in the patches around the cottages, their small white flowers fluttering in the breeze. Elizabeth remembered the harvest, when all the village children went to help dig the crop and carry the potatoes to the pits outside each cottage. That was the only time she had played in the meadow alone.

She walked to the stable yard along the corridor, down the stairway and through the great hall to the passage that led to the back door, the iron tips of her boots sounding against the stone.

Thanking the lad, she stepped into the saddle from the mounting stool, took the reins and set off at a slow walk lest the sound of the horse's hooves disturbed her mother and led to questions later about where she had been. Out of the yard, on the path through the park, she relaxed and let the horse begin to trot, hating the inconvenience of having to ride side-saddle, like a lady. She had been taught to ride that way, but Michael had shown her how to ride bareback, without a saddle, and she preferred that, bunching her skirts up around her knees, careless that her ankles were on show. She had grown up since those days though; her new riding skirt was not full enough to let her ride any other way.

The day was warm now, the sun glowing through clouds that scudded across the sky, the wind a pleasant breeze. Elizabeth rode to the edge of the park, then through the gate into the meadow, turning to check that nobody had seen her.

She wondered what had happened to Michael, whether he had gone away to work like he had said he might, or whether he was still in the village, living in the cottage with his mother and father and nine brothers and sisters. In the years since she'd seen him, she'd had no idea what had happened to him; her friendship with him was a secret, so there was nobody she could ask.

All she knew was that times were hard for the tenants and had been since the potato crop had been lost to blight three years ago. Worry about it had kept her awake at nights until she'd asked Albert about it and he had told her that her father was spending a fortune on road works, which paid the villagers in meal, and there were kitchens handing out free food in Kilkenny, fifteen miles away. Not to worry, he said, nobody would starve.

The village was a couple of miles away, along a rough track. Elizabeth started along it, hoping that she'd meet Michael on the way, that he'd have time for a ride to the riverbank to guddle trout maybe and cook them on an open fire, like they used to do, years ago.

She hoped that he still remembered her, that he had not changed. She knew that, at twenty, he would be considered a young man now, old enough to work alongside his father, old enough to start courting maybe, though she hoped not.

The last time she had seen him, it was the year before

the potatoes had gone bad. He'd gone to work on the wheat harvest with some of the other lads and he had been full of glee because he'd earned 1s 6d for a week's work. He had great plans for the future then, he was going to work in Dublin to earn his fortune, maybe even further afield to England. There was plenty of work and good wages to be made on the railways, he said. Her face must have fallen at the thought of him going away, because he grinned and said that he wasn't going yet, not for a year or two, because his father needed him to help at home. He'd have to wait until his brothers had grown up. They had parted then, with a promise to meet in the spring, but then her father had seen her talking to the village girls and her mother had told her to stay away from them.

There was no way even that she could get a message to him, because her maid did not come from the village, she only went to church there and in any case Elizabeth sensed that her mother would be furious if she found out that she was friendly with a village boy. Lady Roscawl would probably punish Eithne if she found the maid had any part in it and the same went if she asked any of the other maids or the stable-lad.

The first Elizabeth had known of the potato blight was when she overheard the factor telling her father that a few of the tenants were saying that they couldn't pay the rents because the crop was lost and so they'd have to eat the oats they normally sold to pay the rent. Lord Roscawl had told the factor to do the best he could, and although Elizabeth had been concerned she thought that at least the tenants had enough to eat.

Cook stopped serving potatoes at lunch and dinner and

her mother had complained over the inconvenience, because her brothers ate plenty of potatoes, but it had not mattered so much, because there was always a roast, carrots, onions, leeks, things like that as well, with soup and fish and then a sorbet and a pudding of some sort. In any case, her brothers were away at Oxford most of the time.

Her father said it would be the end of them all, with the rates going up tenfold to pay for the Poor Law and that damned lily-livered Peel intent on repealing the Corn Laws. Elizabeth did not know what that meant, beyond that India was involved and her father was angry enough to go red in the face and mutter about the good growing-land that would go to waste. Her father started on about the Chartists and the damned common man not knowing his place any more, and then her mother rang the bell and asked the maid to serve coffee in the drawing-room whilst the butler saw to her father's port. Elizabeth fretted, but was reassured when she heard the factor telling her father that he'd ordered plenty of cornmeal to pay the villagers who worked on the new road.

A year later, Elizabeth had overheard her mother telling her father that the housekeeper had asked if they could take on two village girls as kitchen maids, that she – her mother – did not think that there was need of them, but that the housekeeper had asked particularly because things were tough in the village because of the potatoes. Her father said, damn the village, things were tough at the castle too because the rents had not been paid and the rates had gone up, yet again.

The village girls had not been taken on, and later in the year, when one of the kitchen maids had run off with a stable-lad to America, Elizabeth looked out of her window and saw a queue of village girls at the kitchen door, looking for work. Elizabeth had been thinking about the romance of the elopement, but there was something terribly sad about the long queue of girls, some hardly her age, some even younger, and she prayed that cook would take one or two of them on. In the queue, she saw a couple of girls she recognized; she would have gone to speak to them except the cook would tell her mother and she would get into trouble again.

Once or twice, she had asked Eithne, the maid who worked for her and Sarah, how things were at home; Eithne just pursed her lips and muttered that, with God's help, they would survive. When Albert came home for the holidays, she asked him about it again, and again he said that there was plenty of work on the roads, no need for anyone to go hungry at all.

Out of sight of the castle, she slowed the horse to a walk and undid the pins that held her braided hair to her head, and then the braids themselves. Eithne always did her hair in the morning but Elizabeth hated the constraint, she preferred to wear it long and loose, like the village girls. She put the pins in her pocket, knowing that she would have to do her hair herself on the way back, or else hurt Eithne by letting her know that she had undone her careful creation.

The track reached the top of the hill and in the distance she could see the scattered cottages of Roscawl. She had never been this far by herself before, though she had passed through in the carriage on her way to Kellstraugh, for the dance at Kellstraugh Castle given by her father's cousin.

The cottages had seemed very small then, tiny compared to the castle, too small for one person to live in never mind a whole family. Each cottage was about the size of a stall in the stables, and about the same height. "How do you all fit in?" she'd asked Michael. He had laughed. "I suppose you sleep all alone in your bed?" "Yes," she agreed. "Well, I share mine, my pallet that is, I don't have a bed like yours, just a mattress made of ticking and filled with straw. I share it with all my brothers, and my sisters have another one. You keep warm like that, you don't need so many blankets, nor these daft curtains like you have."

That was another secret she had shared with Michael. Once, when she had already known him for several years, he had said that the castle fascinated him and he would love to see around it. Elizabeth did not understand at first, because the castle was her home, the only home she had ever known, but then he said that he'd only ever seen it from the outside and he'd love to see the inside too. He wanted to see what it was like to be rich.

They waited for weeks and weeks, until nearly the end of summer when her father was away shooting with her brothers and her mother had gone to England with Sarah to visit her own sister, when Elizabeth let Michael in through the door to the gun room at a time when the servants would not see because they were in the servants' hall having their dinner. Silently, they went through the great hall, past the main stairway where portraits hung of all the Lords Roscawl and most of the Ladies, to the dining-room, with its mahogany and silver, the drawing-room with its red flock and velvet, the little salon with its spinet and piano, the smoking-room and the library, the formal rooms where her parents entertained.

Michael was astonished by it all, astonished most of all by Elizabeth's own room, with its child-sized four-poster with curtains, the softly upholstered chairs, the wardrobe that held all her dresses, the shelves of books and the little table that held her collection of porcelain figures.

He bounced up and down on her bed. "It's fantastic," he said. "Unbelievable. If I hadn't seen it with my own eyes, I'd never've believed that anyone could live like this."

Elizabeth shrugged.

He picked up the bell by her bedside and began to ring it, before she flew over and stopped him. "That's for the maid," she shrieked, knocking it out of his hand.

He looked at her in amazement.

"Quick," she said, bundling him under the bed as, far away, she could hear Eithne's footsteps climbing the stairs. Elizabeth met her in the hall. "I dropped the bell," she said, "I'm sorry. I didn't mean to call you."

She made Michael wait for ten minutes, until she was sure the coast was clear, before they crept down the stairs again, to leave by the side door. Just before they reached it, Michael pulled her back, then ran into the drawing-room and rang each bell in turn before he grabbed her by the hand and ran outside, laughing madly. He put his finger to his lips as they listened below a window as the servants came, asking each other what was happening and who had rung all the bells?

Elizabeth was terrified that they would be discovered. Michael just chuckled, careless of the chaos he had caused. All the way back to the meadow, he shook his head. "Daft," he muttered. "Just daft. You just ring a bell and people come running."

*   *   *

Elizabeth smiled to herself at the memory as she drew closer to the village. She was well past the castle home farm now, approaching the small fields, patches really, where the potatoes had grown before the blight. She had supposed that there would be something else growing instead, but the strips of earth lay neglected, only a weed breaking the surface, here and there.

She noticed the change first as she passed the bacon curer's, which she remembered for its rich smells of smoke and brine that wafted into the carriage as it passed. The smokehouse was deserted, a plank nailed across the door, and there was a crow's nest in the chimney that used to belch smoke, day and night. The street was quiet, though it was hardly that, just a track between the houses that was usually full of people, talking and laughing. The cottage doors had always been open in the old days, but now they were closed firmly to discourage visitors.

Elizabeth felt a chill and shivered slightly.

There was an air of despair, of desolation about the place. It was worse, much worse, than she expected it to be. In the pit of her stomach, she felt the beginnings of dread. She had believed Albert's assurances, but now she doubted what he had said. She stopped beside the Inn, where O'Callaghan, the gombeen-man, who Michael hated almost as much as he hated Fraser, the factor, used to lend money at exorbitant rates and buy any spare produce for a pittance. That was closed too, the door boarded and charred at the edges, as if someone had tried to set fire to it.

She rode on slowly, past a cottage where an old woman

came out with a bucket of water, pausing when she saw her and then shrieking in Irish like a dervish. Elizabeth urged the horse on, ignoring her. She did not understand Irish, beyond a few words that she suspected were naughty which Michael had taught her.

Michael's cottage was, she knew, at the end of the village, marked out by the cartwheels balanced against the walls. His father owned the only cart in the village; he kept the wheels for spares.

When she reached it she dismounted and walked to the door, calling out and then knocking when nobody came.

She noticed the silence then, for the first time, the silence that hung over the village like a shroud.

She waited, listening for a sound. When none came, she knocked again, then heard a soft shuffling before the door slowly opened.

A woman stood there, Michael's mother, she supposed, though she looked very old and thin, with wispy grey hair that fell to her shoulders in greasy strands. She peered at Elizabeth for a moment before recognition came into her eyes. "Are ye the young lady from the castle, Miss? What are you doing here, Miss? D'ye not know we've the fever?"

Elizabeth swallowed. "Please, I want to see Michael."

"He's away on the roads, Miss. Away now before you catch the fever."

"Please, can you ask him to come to see me?"

The woman waved her arm; Elizabeth moved back a step.

"Please, tell him to come and see me."

"He'll not be back before nightfall."

"Tell him to come then. Tell him to meet me in the

meadow. I'll wait for him. Please," Elizabeth said, "I must see him."

The woman seemed about to say something before she nodded her head once. "Pity's sake, Miss. Get away from here before you catch the fever."

"Please," Elizabeth said, "tell him I didn't know how bad things are. Tell him I'll try to help."

The woman did not hear her, she had already closed the door.

Chapter 2

Back at the castle, Elizabeth sat for a long time at her dressing-table, her head in her hands, then she rang the bell and asked Eithne to bring water so that she could wash. Mechanically, she stripped off her riding clothes, then scrubbed herself all over before she dressed for dinner and then sat down whilst Eithne fussed over her hair.

"There's fever in Roscawl, Eithne, isn't there?" she asked her, watching the maid's face as she carefully combed out her plaits.

Eithne flinched. "So they say, Miss. I wouldn't know. I haven't been to the village, but for Mass on Sunday. But the priest said a special prayer for the sick, and the church was half empty. But ye needn't fear, it'll not reach the castle."

Elizabeth watched her intently. "Has the doctor been?"

Eithne stifled a bitter laugh. "No money to pay him, Miss Elizabeth. Everybody's afraid o' the fever, the doctor as much as anyone else."

"How bad is it?"

Eithne pursed her lips. "People're dying, Miss. But then, they've been dying in the village for years now, ever since the potatoes went bad."

Elizabeth looked down, so that the maid would not see

the shock of realization in her eyes. Albert's words echoed in her head: *"Not to worry, nobody will starve"*. Guilt overwhelmed her when she thought of the life she led at the castle, of the table groaning with food. There the lack of potatoes had been an inconvenience; she'd assumed that when the potato crop had failed the villagers ate something else, that the loss of the crop meant a degree of hardship, no more than that. It was hard to believe that people had actually died.

Eithne began to twist her hair into a chignon, pulling her face up. Elizabeth blinked to clear the tears that had sprung to her eyes.

"How many?" she asked, in a small voice. She was afraid of the answer, but she had to ask.

"What, Miss?"

"How many have died?"

"I don't rightly know, Miss. Old McKerragher and his missus, some o' the wains. A whole family went to the fever a month past, one of the lads said."

"But I thought, I thought there were oats to eat. There's meal from the road and you can get food if you go to Kilkenny," she blurted.

Eithne looked wistful for a moment. "There's meal from the road, right enough, but it's not enough. And the oats're not enough either. See, plant potatoes and you'll grow enough to feed a family for a year. Plant oats and there'll only be enough to last weeks, a month or two at most." She finished putting pins in Elizabeth's hair and waited for her approval.

Elizabeth nodded, hardly looking at it. "Your family, Eithne, are your family all right?"

Eithne smiled. "Thank the Lord. They're in Cork city, Miss, and it's kind of you to ask. But they've my money and my sister's, and my brother in America sends them some every month. It's not much, but it keeps them fed, just about."

At dinner, Elizabeth sat and toyed with the poached salmon on the plate before her. Her mother, dressed in a gown of pale grey silk, wore the Roscawl emeralds around her neck. She always wore jewels in the evening, and the emeralds were particularly special. The size of small duck's eggs, they were surrounded by diamonds on a rope of white gold. The jewels glowed in the light shed by the candles balanced in the silver candelabra that stood in the centre of the table.

Elizabeth's mother believed in keeping up appearances, so they always ate formally in the dining-room whether her father was there or not.

Lady Roscawl finished her fish, and the butler took the plates away, Elizabeth's hardly touched, and replaced them with others for the roast beef.

Elizabeth coughed. During the meal, she was supposed to keep up polite conversation, but so far she had said nothing.

Her mother looked at her.

"There's fever in the village," Elizabeth blurted. "And people have died."

Lady Roscawl pursed her lips, but said nothing. The butler continued to serve the beef and then, from a tureen, carrots and peas. There were little dough puddings shaped like potatoes and a rich gravy made with wine.

"There's fever in the village," Elizabeth said again.

Lady Roscawl picked up her knife and fork and began to eat.

"Didn't you hear what I said?" Elizabeth asked.

Her mother paused. "I heard perfectly well what you said," she replied, in a low voice.

"Well, why didn't you say something?" Elizabeth was aware that she was being terribly rude.

Her mother balanced her knife and fork carefully at the side of her plate. "I do not think that what you said is a suitable subject for a dinner-table conversation," she said tersely.

"But it's true! People are dying!"

Lady Roscawl sighed and looked at the ceiling, where plaster cherubs flew against a painted blue sky. "Elizabeth," she said, "for the last time, this is not a subject for discussion at the dinner table. I would be obliged if you would let me continue to eat my meal."

Elizabeth hesitated for a moment, then she placed her knife and fork together over the uneaten beef and rose and left the table.

"Elizabeth!"

She ignored her mother. As the butler opened the door for her, she detected a look of understanding in his eyes, or she imagined that she did.

In her room, Elizabeth sat down in front of the mirror and did her hair herself. Although she knew that her mother was furious with her, she also knew that she was too much of a lady to do anything about it.

After night had fallen, she dressed warmly in an old skirt

and riding jacket, then she crept along the corridor and downstairs through the still warm kitchen, where she let herself out into the kitchen garden.

The sky was clear and the moon had risen. Elizabeth kept to the shadows until she was out of the kitchen garden, then she walked along the wall until she reached the path to the meadow, where she began to run. She had never been out of the castle at night before, and she could not imagine what her parents would do if they found out. Yet she had to see Michael, to tell him that she hadn't known how bad things were, but now that she did, she would do what she could to help.

As she approached the meadow, she could not see him. I should have known, she thought. I should have come before. She stopped for a moment, sick with guilt, then she reminded herself about Albert's assurances. He would not have known either, she thought. He would not have lied to her, not Albert, the brother who had been so kind to her. She doubted that even her father knew; he surely would not let people die for the lack of food when there was so much at the castle.

She would have come before, except at first she was afraid of getting the village children into trouble and then, for the past year, there had been no time. She shuddered when she realized how selfish, how careless she had been, but she would make up for it now. She had not meant to be thoughtless, she cared very much, it was just that she had never imagined, for a moment, that things were so bad that people were dying.

She climbed over the gate and whistled softly.

The branches of the willow moved, and Michael walked

towards her. She gasped with surprise, then stared at him. He was much taller than she remembered him, and leaner, though he still walked with the same easy stride.

"Hallo, little *mavourneen*," he said softly. "I hear you've been looking for me." He carried a jacket over his shoulder, and his shirt was ripped and darned. In the light of the moon the skin of his face was dark, his features rugged.

"It's been a long time," he said. "What is it, four years? I thought you'd forgotten me."

"I…" I would never have forgotten you, she was going to say, but something stopped her. "Michael, the way things've been, I didn't know. I'd no idea."

"I waited, you know. I waited here to see you for days that spring, but you never came."

"I … my father saw me talking to two of the girls and he … my governess was watching me, and…" Her voice tailed off into helplessness. "Michael, about the potatoes. I didn't know how bad things were, truly I didn't. I only found out when I went to the village today."

He shrugged and walked to the wall, where he sat down. She was remembering the games she used to play with him, the laughter and the fun. He looked at her intently and as he did so his expression changed. "You didn't know," he echoed her.

"No. I knew the potatoes had gone bad, but I thought you had oats to eat. Albert said there was work on the road as well, and food from the kitchen in Kilkenny. He said there was plenty of Poor Relief, that nobody would go hungry."

"Poor Relief?" he laughed bitterly. "Is that what you call

21

it? Three-quarters of a pound of grain for a day's work? Slavery is what I call it."

"Michael, I…"

"My father died of the fever, but the fact is he'd have died anyway because there was no food for him. Your friend the factor banned him from working on the road because he said Da had given him cheek. That was my father, mind, who in all his life never had a bad word to say of anybody, least of all your own da. D'you know what his last words were? He told my ma not to mourn him, that it was a blessing…" Michael laughed bitterly again and stared at her. "That's how bad things are, Elizabeth. People are saying the fever's a blessing because it's a quick death, better than starvation."

She looked away to hide the tears that sprung to her eyes. "I'm sorry," she said, softly.

"Sorry?"

"I'm still your friend, Michael. That hasn't changed."

He shook his head. "The times have changed. I know my place now, not that I didn't always, but I thought you were different, see? One of us, not one of these heathen devils who complains about the Poor Law Rate and the rents not being paid."

"I am. Michael, I'm so sorry, so very sorry."

His voice was so cold that she shivered. "Being sorry doesn't help."

He jumped off the wall and walked away with long, angry strides, leaving her stunned by his anger, crying sour salt tears that stung her cheeks.

Shoulders slumped, she turned and began the walk back to the castle. The wind picked up, brushing the grass.

Elizabeth felt its gentle breath dry the tears in her eyes.

Michael had been hurt, she realized, because she had not gone to see him, because he thought that she didn't care. He did not understand how strict her mother was, how closely she had been watched, how she was afraid not so much of getting into trouble herself, but of getting the village children into trouble on her behalf. I didn't know, she told herself, again. It's not my fault.

An owl called out, its cry plaintive above the sound of the wind. I know now, she realized. Now that I do, I can do something to help.

A mile away from the castle, Michael stopped and put his jacket on. The anger that had made him hot had gone, to be replaced by a dull pain and the memory of Elizabeth's face, along with the knowledge that he had hurt her.

He had not meant to; when his mother told him that Elizabeth had come looking for him he had been filled with joy that she still remembered; that, after the years apart, she still thought about him. All along the road to the castle, he had been thinking about her, about what he would say to her. He didn't want to tell her the truth, that each day was a struggle, that sometimes he was so tired that when he went to sleep he wondered if he would ever have the strength to get up again. He wanted to tell her a lie that, although things were hard they were managing, that they still had hope that better times would come.

In the village, hope was something that had all but vanished. After three years of blight, even the priest had stopped saying that better times would come.

At first, they thought that the potatoes would grow the

next year, but then the blight came again, the same black blight with the bitter smell that swept over the village from the diseased potato beds.

That was when men began to leave to find work in Dublin or further afield. A few lucky ones had the boat fare to Liverpool, where they went to find work in factories or on the railway, but Michael had nothing, only the boots his cousin had given him. And, once he had walked to Dublin, even they were done in.

There was no work in the city, the rumour that said otherwise was wrong. After a week without food, living only on rainwater, he had turned and walked back barefoot, careless of the cuts on the soles of his feet.

For a while, they'd given out food, outdoor relief they called it, in Kilkenny, fifteen miles away. Although it took all day to walk there and back, the village people had gone to be fed with a bowl of something called stirabout, a mix of meal and rice.

It had hurt their dignity to accept charity, but they had gone nevertheless. Now that they had stopped giving out stirabout, he did not know if the meagre rations he got for working on the road would be enough to feed his family.

His dream, his wildest dream, had been to go to America. When he was young, playing with Elizabeth, he had wanted to tell her, had wanted her to agree that she would come too. Although he knew that there was a difference between them, that she was rich and he was poor, he thought that in time he would bridge that distance, make enough money so that he could support her, maybe not exactly like a lady, but near enough so that she would not notice too much of a difference.

The dream seemed hollow now. Childish and foolish. He had watched her walking towards the field. Even in the thin light of the moon, she looked healthy and well fed. The clothes that she wore would cost a month's wages or more – he could never afford even to keep her clad.

His friend Sean had joined the Young Irelanders in Cork. The Young Irelanders had vowed to fight the landlords for Ireland; Michael might have joined too if he thought they had any chance of success.

To survive the potato blight, they'd had to eat the oats that were normally sold to pay the rent. Michael's father had managed to pay the rent the first year, but not the second. He had not lived to see the third.

Just two days before, the factor, Fraser, had posted notices threatening eviction on anyone whose rent wasn't paid, knowing full well that the reason rent was not paid was that the oats were the only food in the village.

Michael remembered the day his father, Francis O'Shea, had gone out to work on the Committee road. (The road was being paid for by the Poor Law to give the people a chance to put some food into their mouths.) Fraser had been there and he had asked why the O'Sheas' rent was not paid. Michael's father said that he could not pay it because he had to use the grain to feed his children. To Fraser, that was cheek, enough to tell Francis that there would be no work for him on the road. Fraser said that the Poor Law roads would provide food enough, the rent still had to be paid.

Michael remembered his father's face when he had come home that day and he felt a wild anger when he thought about it. It was that anger that had made him hurt Elizabeth. Fraser worked for her father, after all.

Every morning for two years now, he had risen before dawn and walked to wherever it was that the roads were being built, waited in line for the bit of paper that would entitle him to grain at the end of the day and then gone to work. He earned three-quarters of a pound of Indian corn-meal some days, some days a full pound if the overseers were feeling generous. Together with the oats, that was all his family had to live on. They did have a cow, but her milk went to feed the wains, the little ones.

He walked over the hill before the village and saw his cottage at the end of the row, the thin smoke from the chimney streaking the night sky. He was the man of the house now, the one responsible for the family's survival.

Though, deep inside he remembered Elizabeth, other thoughts now crowded his mind.

Like what was his family going to eat today, and would Fraser really evict them, if the rent was not paid? And, if so, how he would ever find the money to pay it, *and* keep everyone fed.

Chapter 3

Elizabeth woke up with a dead feeling in her stomach. She had hardly slept until dawn and then she had fallen into a deep, dreamless sleep. She lay in bed for a moment or two before the memories of the night before came back, the dull ache of the hurt returned.

Eithne opened the door and came in with her morning tea.

"It's a lovely day, Miss Elizabeth," she said, opening the curtains to blinding sunlight.

Elizabeth blinked against the light and thanked the maid.

"Will ye be going out riding again?"

"No … yes … I'm not sure," she said. "Have you seen my mother this morning?"

"The Lady's staying abed, Brigid said." Brigid was her mother's maid. "She's not feeling so well today."

Elizabeth waited until the maid had gone, and then rose slowly and sat at the window seat, sipping her tea. The sun shone brightly over the park; birds sang and she could see the swans on the lake.

She was thinking about what Michael had said, wondering what she could do. Although her parents were distant figures, she loved them, or so she thought. Though Fraser's hatred of the tenants was well known, she could not believe that her father would wilfully let people die, not when there was plenty of food in the castle stores.

The day passed slowly. Elizabeth read for a while, then played the piano. In the evening, after she had dined alone, she told Eithne that she would go to bed early, then she lay awake thinking.

When the castle was silent, she got up again and dressed quickly and then walked, in stockinged feet, through the kitchen to the big larder where food was stored. There were sacks of flour and sugar, rounds of cheese and butter and whole hams hung from the ceiling, slowly curing in the dry air.

She thought for a moment and then went outside, pausing to put her riding boots on, and into the stables where she called softly to Jamie, the stable-lad, who slept in the loft above the horses.

He woke up, afraid at first until she told him that it was only her.

"Quickly," she said, "I need to take the pony trap. I'm going to the village."

"Why … why, Miss Elizabeth? It's the dead of night, for pity's sake."

"They're hungry in the village," she said, simply. "I'm going to take them some food."

"Ye'll have me the sack, so ye will. Enough of yer daft ideas and away to bed with ye."

She glared at him. "If you don't help me, Jamie, I'll sack you."

"Ye would not."

"I would so."

He scratched his head and muttered something, then went to a stall and brought out the pony and then wheeled the trap over.

"Ye'll get caught, so ye will."

Elizabeth was thinking. There were twelve cottages in the village. She was wondering how much food she could take without getting found out.

"Ye're serious, aren't ye?"

"I've never been more serious in my life, Jamie."

"Ye could take the Poor Law meal, I suppose."

"What's that?"

"It's the meal Fraser hands out, for the Poor Law work. There's a shed full o' it. Stacked to the rafters. He'd never notice if a sack or two went missing."

She thought for a moment longer. The castle storeroom, next to the larder, was stacked to the rafters too.

"If Fraser found out, there'd be hell to pay."

Jamie grinned. "Aye, but the bastard's hoarding it, see? It's Poor Law meal, meant for the people, and he's handing it out as if it's his own personal gift. He's not supposed to hoard it. He's meant to give it out. He can hardly complain if we do it for him, can he?"

"Can you get into the shed, Jamie?"

"Aye."

Elizabeth went back into the castle, returning with a round of cheese and a couple of hams and a big knife to cut them. By then, Jamie had the cart hitched up and four sacks of meal loaded on it.

"I'll come with you, Miss Elizabeth."

She shook her head. She was better to go alone.

*   *   *

Every night for a week, Elizabeth went to bed early and then got up again and took the cart to the village, where she left some meal and a bit of cheese or ham outside every cottage. The cook had not noticed anything, she thought, and Jamie was filling sacks with earth and stacking them in the shed so that Fraser would not realize that any were gone.

Elizabeth had no idea what happened to the food after she had left it, but she knew that she could not live with herself if she did nothing at all.

At the beginning of the second week, she dared to ask Eithne how things were. The maid stared at her for a moment before she spoke. "There's been a miracle, Miss Elizabeth. There's an angel leaving food outside the houses, every day for the past week."

"Is that right?" Elizabeth asked her.

"It's what folks are saying, Miss, right enough."

Michael stopped her that night, as she was driving the empty cart back to the castle.

"I guessed it was you," he said, once she had recovered from the surprise of him suddenly appearing before her.

She looked away. His last words to her had been so bitter that she was still hurting.

"Elizabeth, I'm sorry. The things I said, I was angry. I thought you'd forgotten. I thought you didn't care."

She looked back at him. "Of course I care. I just didn't know."

"Thanks for the food."

"It's nothing. It's what anybody would do, if they knew."

He shook his head. "This land's full of people who know

and do nothing. Take a man like your father. He knows, but he's done nothing these past three years."

She flinched. "My father's paid the rates to buy the meal."

"Yes, and he left it in the hands of a man like Fraser. Yon's been selling Poor Law meal in Cork, y'know. Making money out of the starving. I hope he rots in hell for it!"

Elizabeth flinched at his anger. "I doubt my father knows that," she said softly.

"Any case," Michael said, "I just came to thank you, and to tell you to be careful. Be very careful, Elizabeth."

"I am very careful," she said softly.

He moved a step closer and involuntarily her breath quickened. "You've done enough for a while, *mavourneen*. There's food enough to last till the end of the week. Have a rest. You deserve it."

Her eyes flashed. "What about you, Michael? When will you ever have a rest?"

"Ach." His mouth tightened and he turned away. "I'll rest when all this is over." He looked at her closely for a moment. "You reckon your dad doesn't know what Fraser's doing?"

"I don't think so. I don't think he'd let anyone starve."

"Well, can you tell him, *mavourneen*? Can you tell him that Fraser's not giving out the meal like he should, that he's selling some of it in Cork?"

Elizabeth was thinking of the distant, vaguely friendly figure of her father. He would be back soon, she knew, once parliament was in its summer recess.

"I'll do what I can, Michael."

He smiled, and, very gently, brushed his hand against her cheek.

She watched him walk away, as the skin of her face burned.

When Lord Roscawl came back, Elizabeth's mother rose from her bed for the first time in a week. She treated Elizabeth as if the row had never happened. Although Elizabeth tried to join in the conversation at the dinner table, both her parents ignored her, as they usually did, noticing her only at the end of the meal, when she excused herself.

After she had left the dining-room, she heard her father remark to her mother that she looked well and that she had grown; her mother said that there was still a wild streak in her, that it would be best for them all if they could find her a husband so that she could settle down. "I think I'll take her to London, introduce her to some civilized people. We want her to marry well, don't we?"

Her father harrumphed.

Elizabeth's blood ran cold at the very thought of it.

The following day, she waited until her father was in his study and then went to see him, pausing when she heard voices behind the closed door.

"The best thing, Milord, would be to get rid of the lot of them." The voice was that of Fraser, the factor. She had not seen him come in, he must have been waiting in her father's study.

Her father said something in a low voice which she could not catch.

"The whole village is in arrears, Milord, and there's no chance of the rents being paid this term. And you'll have to keep feeding them."

Elizabeth leaned closer to the door.

"It's a damnable thing, Fraser," her father was saying. "I don't like the thought of kicking them out, though. They've been here as long as we have, most of them."

"The rents are a pittance, even when they're paid. You'd be best rid of them, and put the land under sheep."

"I'll think about it," her father said. Elizabeth scampered along the corridor and hid in an alcove while the factor walked out, a look of anger on his face.

After lunch, when her mother went upstairs for a nap, her father returned to his study. Diffidently, Elizabeth knocked at the door and waited for his command to enter.

"Why, Elizabeth," he said, "what a pleasant surprise. Sit down, my dear, and tell me what you've been getting up to."

Gingerly, she balanced herself on the edge of a deep leather chair. Now that she was in her father's presence, her courage deserted her and she said nothing, frantically searching for the right words.

"What's on your mind, my dear?" he smiled. "If you don't tell me, I'll never know."

She coughed. "It's the people, Father, the tenants. They're starving in the village, and they've been dying of the fever."

He frowned. "They aren't starving, Elizabeth. They're given meal by the Poor Law. You mustn't believe what you read in the papers. It's not as bad as people make out."

"But it is!" she blurted. "Fraser has the Poor Law meal, but he's not giving it out like he's supposed to. If he doesn't like someone, they don't get the meal, and you know he doesn't like any of the tenants. And he's been selling it in Cork!"

Lord Roscawl's eyes narrowed. "And how do you know all this, Elizabeth? Who have you been speaking to?"

She looked away. "Nobody, Father. I just hear things that people are saying."

"What things, Elizabeth? Are the servants saying that? Who?"

She looked down at her hands.

"You must tell me, Elizabeth. If that is true, then we must do something about it. And if not, it is a vicious slander." His voice softened a tone. "Come now, you can tell me. I know you used to talk to the village children. Is it one of them who told you?"

Elizabeth flinched. "I … no, Father. I was out for a ride and I heard two men talking."

"Who were they? Were they tenants?"

"I don't know, Father. I didn't recognize them."

Lord Roscawl smiled. "You mustn't believe everything you hear, my dear. It is true that times are hard, and there are some nasty men who are trying to turn that hardship to their own ends."

"But can't we do something, Father? Give them more meal, pay for a doctor maybe?"

He smiled. "We are already doing enough, my dear. The rates are several times what they were a few years ago. The government had devoted a great deal of money to the relief effort and as for our own tenants, I think that maybe the time has come when they would be better off elsewhere. They have so little land, my dear, that at the best of times they are struggling to make ends meet. I don't want you to worry your head about it. And if you hear any more talk, tell me."

Knowing that she was being dismissed, Elizabeth rose and walked out of her father's study. Her thoughts were whirling between what she had seen in the village and what Michael had said, and, on the other hand, her father's bland reassurances.

Chapter 4

That night, Elizabeth lay awake thinking, as the moon tracked a path across the dark Irish sky. Michael's face, his skin weather-beaten, his features rugged, drifted before her. He had not been lying to her about the factor, she knew that.

After she slept, she dreamed about him. They were children again, playing in the fields; she was happy as she had never been before or since. Then, when she went indoors for her dinner, her mother and father were waiting for her. They told her that she had to go to London; she would never see Michael again. Elizabeth woke up with a feeling of desolate loss.

In the morning, she asked Jamie to saddle her horse, then she rode out over the moors to the place where the Committee road was being dug. It was a beautiful day, the sun was shining brightly and the wind had faded to a whisper. Elizabeth watched the village men and boys at work on the road for a while, then she turned and headed for home.

Michael saw her. He did not dare pause in his labours, because Fraser was watching. There were many things on his mind, most of all the threat of eviction if the rent was not paid. Two of his brothers were old enough to work with him on the roads, but the meal they earned was hardly enough to feed the rest of his brothers and sisters and his mother. The choice he faced was harsh: to sell the oats and pay the rent, but starve, or to keep the oats to eat and get evicted.

He could think of no solution.

That night, Elizabeth slipped out of the castle when everyone was asleep. In the stables, she woke Jamie, then she took the cart and a couple of sacks of meal to the village. She also took a cheese and a ham from the kitchen store room, which she cut up, leaving a bit outside every cottage with the meal.

Michael was waiting for her just outside the village. She got a shock when he stood up from the hedgerow where he had been sitting.

"It's been a week," she said.

"Aye." In the moonlight, she could see that he was smiling at her. She jumped off the cart, took the horse by the reins and they walked along the track together.

"How are you?"

He shrugged; he was only wearing a thin cotton shirt and she worried that he might get cold. "The food you bring, that helps. See, not everybody can work the road. The widow Flanagan, she's only got daughters. Keeping her alive, so you are."

"I told my father about Fraser."

"And?"

Elizabeth hesitated. "He wanted proof," she said, slowly.

"All he's got to do is ask the merchants in Cork."

They walked in silence for a while. Elizabeth sensed there was something on Michael's mind. She asked him what.

"It's the rent," he said.

"What about it?"

"Well, to pay the rent, I'd have to sell the oats, but I need the oats to eat, because we don't get enough on the roads. Fraser's threatening to evict us if we don't pay the rent."

Elizabeth's heart quickened; she had heard Fraser saying that in her father's study. "I'll bring you food."

"Yes, but…" He was thinking that Elizabeth would not be there for ever, that she would go away.

"But what?"

"You won't always be here, *mavourneen*."

"I don't want to ever leave Ireland, Michael."

He smiled sadly to himself. He did not know much about the gentry, but one thing that he did know was that a girl like Elizabeth did not have much choice about her life.

"How much is the rent, Michael?"

"One pound, five shillings. It's not due for a couple of months, but he put the notices up at Whitsun."

Elizabeth was thinking that she had no idea of what £1 5s even looked like. She had never even seen money; anything she needed was ordered and paid for by her father. She did not know even if it was a lot of money or a little; she thought hard, then remembered her mother saying to Sarah that the material for one of her trousseau outfits was very expensive, that it cost a guinea a yard. If dress fabric could cost a guinea a yard, she supposed that £1 5s for a year's rent was not so much.

"I don't know what I can do, Michael."

He stopped walking, turned and smiled at her.

"*Mavourneen*, you don't have to do anything. You're doing enough already."

They parted at the bend in the track. Michael stood there for a long time, watching Elizabeth until she was safely within the boundaries of the castle. Then he turned and headed home. He had been going to the river to try to guddle some trout, when he'd seen Elizabeth, but the trout would have to wait until tomorrow. Elizabeth had left plenty of food, in any case.

Michael was a dreamer. On the way home, he dreamed that he went to America, that he made plenty of money there and came back with enough to offer to marry Elizabeth. The dream was forlorn though, he realized, as he reached the cottage. By the time he'd made enough money, Lord Roscawl would already have married Elizabeth to someone else. And, besides, a lord would never let his daughter marry a Catholic peasant.

Indoors, he put the food she'd left away, then he took his clothes off and slipped under the blanket of the pallet he shared with his brothers. Years ago, when he'd gone to Dublin to find work, he'd gone to a Young Ireland meeting. There was anger throughout the country; there had been for hundreds of years, ever since the English invasion. The Young Irelanders talked of a rising, there were rumours that they were going to rise now. Michael doubted if the rising would be successful, if it would ever come to anything at all; the hunger had sapped the will of the people, made them too weak and tired to fight.

With the other young men of the village, he had talked, vowed vengeance against the landlords who'd milked them of every last penny in rent, then turned their backs when the potatoes went bad. But the problem was that they had nothing to seek vengeance with, no guns or anything like that. Only their bare hands, and even the little strength they had was used up road-digging, to earn the meal that kept them alive.

Michael had never hated anybody, it was not in his nature to hate. In the years since the potato blight, though, he had come to hate Fraser, for denying his father the chance of work on the roads. The denial had, he knew, contributed to his father's death.

Sometimes, he could no longer see a future for himself in Ireland, in the land of hunger and death. The only future he could see was in America. He fell asleep, dreaming of that. And also of Elizabeth.

Elizabeth was in the music room the next day, playing the piano, when Eithne came in. She had not called the maid, she wondered why she was there. Eithne stood before her, fumbling with the skirt of her apron.

"What is it, Eithne?" she asked her.

"Oh, Miss Elizabeth, there's terrible trouble in the kitchen. Cook says there's been food stolen and she says she's going to tell Milady about it."

"What food?"

"I'm not sure, Miss. Cook says a cheese and a ham. She's got all the girls down there, and she says if the thief doesn't confess, she'll tell Milady and they'll get the constables in."

Elizabeth thought for a moment.

"Cook says, if the thief doesn't confess, then she'll sack all the girls," Eithne said. "Oh, Miss, we need our jobs, so we do. We've got families to support."

Elizabeth thanked Eithne, then she got up and went down to the kitchen. Cook was standing there, her arms folded belligerently, as the kitchen maids and housemaids stood in a line before her. All of them looked distraught, some were in tears.

"Why, Miss Elizabeth," Cook said, "what on earth are you doing down here?"

Elizabeth smiled. When she had been younger, she had considered it a great treat to go down to the kitchen, where Cook would serve her a glass of milk and a piece of freshly-baked fruit cake. She loved the big room for its warmth and its smell of food.

"Can I have a word with you, please, Mrs Murphy?"

Cook hesitated, but Elizabeth led her firmly to the small office off the kitchen. She closed the door.

"I took the cheese and the ham," she said.

Cook frowned. "But, Miss Elizabeth, what on earth for?"

"They're starving in the village. It'll never be missed. You know that."

"But…"

"I took it last night, in the cart. If you don't believe me, you can ask Jamie."

Cook looked thoughtful. She had been with the Roscawls all her life, first as a kitchen maid and then as a cook. She had been widowed years ago; Elizabeth knew that her sons were in America. She was a kindly woman, but strict with the maids who worked under her.

"You must not fire anybody. If you want to blame some-one, blame me."

Cook sighed, then smiled. "You should have told me,

Miss Elizabeth. I know times are hard. I do what I can. I send a basket to the priest every day."

"I'm sorry if I caused any trouble."

"Don't be, Miss Elizabeth. You were just trying to help. Bless you."

Outside the kitchen, Elizabeth paused to gather her courage, then she walked along to her father's study. The door was open; Lord Roscawl was sitting at his desk, reading a copy of *The Times*. Elizabeth knocked gently, went in when he looked up and smiled at her.

Lord Roscawl put the paper down. "It's a dastardly state of affairs," he said.

"What is?"

"A lot of stuff and nonsense, my dear, but you don't have to trouble your pretty head about it."

"About what?"

"These dashed troublemakers, O'Brien Smith and his mob, they're up to no good again. Rabble-rousing and so on, but you don't have to worry about it, my dear, the government's got precautions well in hand."

Elizabeth smiled and sat down.

"What can I do for you, my dear?" her father asked her.

Elizabeth hesitated, fumbled to find the right words. "I'd like some money, Father."

"Money? What on earth do you need money for?"

Elizabeth's mind performed somersaults. Travelling gypsies usually came round in the summer, selling ribbons and trinkets. "If the pedlars come," she said, slowly.

"Tsk. You shouldn't be encouraging these people. Lawless nuisances, they are. You don't need money, Elizabeth.

Women don't. Anything you need, I pay for. You know that."

"I'd like to have some," she insisted.

He frowned, reached into a box on his desk, handed her a couple of coins. "There's two shillings, if you must. But I don't know what on earth you need it for."

Elizabeth took the coins and thanked him; she could not think of a reason to ask him for more.

Later, Eithne was helping her dress for dinner when she asked the maid how much £1 5s was.

Eithne cocked her head to one side. "That's a lot of money, to the likes of us, Miss Elizabeth. Likes of me, I get paid two guineas for the year."

Elizabeth thought for a moment. "How much do my dresses cost?"

"Well, I don't rightly know, Miss. It depends on the material. Cotton's cheaper than velvet. But I was going to say, Miss, that money, it's not much to a man like your father. His Lordship's rich, so he is."

"Do I have anything that's worth £1 5s?"

Eithne smiled. "Surely you do, Miss Elizabeth. Just about everything you have. That gold locket you have, it's worth several times that."

Elizabeth was thinking how unfair it was, that she and her family were rich, whereas Eithne and the village people were poor. She said that; Eithne just smiled, and said that it was the will of the Lord, that was the way things were.

Elizabeth wondered how she could accept it so easily.

That night, Elizabeth waited until the castle was silent and then she crept out. In the stables, she saddled her horse herself, because she did not want to wake Jamie, then she rode to the river, where she knew that Michael would be. She tied the reins of her horse to a branch of an oak tree, then she walked to the bank, where he was lying with his arms deep in the water. He was trying to guddle a trout, she knew. She'd watched him guddling trout years ago and knew not to disturb him, so she sat down silently besides him. He acknowledged her with a nod.

Michael's face was rapt with concentration. The light of the moon reflected from the river, outlining his features. Elizabeth thought how good-looking he was, how strong. The famine had turned him into a man.

Michael sighed inwardly. He had been thinking of America. His cousin Donal was there; his family had managed to scrape together the fare and he had written to them and told them that he had a job already. Donal was lucky; his father had a small inn in Cork and the family were not dependent upon the land for their livelihood. Michael knew that if he asked his uncle, Donal's father, to help with the rent he would, if he could. The trouble was that he was proud, he did not want to ask anyone to help. He wanted to be like Donal, to have a job, to be able to earn a livelihood of his own. He had thought of writing to Donal and asking him to lend him the money for his fare to America, but he could not afford a stamp and he did not have pen or paper. Also, he did not want to be beholden, even to Donal.

The waters stirred; he sensed a fish approach, tensed to catch it. When it was within reach, he grabbed it, lifted it up but the scales were slippery and it twisted out of his grip, landing back in the river with a plop.

Michael swore. The fish had been a trout, a big one. It would have been a good meal for his family, for their neighbours, the Ryans, as well. Young Joe Ryan sometimes trapped rabbits and when he did he always gave some to the O'Sheas.

"I'm sorry," Elizabeth said. She felt his loss.

He smiled, shook the water from his arms and tore off dock leaves to dry them. "Don't be," he said, "there's always another one." He was thinking that she looked very beautiful in the moonlight, her fair hair like wisps of gold around her face.

Elizabeth reached into her pocket. "I was thinking," she said, "about your rent. I want you to have this. You can sell it. It's worth more than one pound, five shillings."

Michael looked, saw a heavy gold locket on a thin gold chain. For a moment, his love for Elizabeth surged, then his pride took over.

"Keep your gold," he said coldly. "I don't need it."

"But Michael…"

He turned and walked quickly away. He did not want her to see how red his face was, how ashamed he was to be in such a position that he needed her charity. In his dreams, he wanted to be the one to give her gold, whatever she wanted or needed.

She began to walk after him. "Michael?"

"Go away, Elizabeth. Go back to your castle."

She followed him, but he broke into a run, easily outpacing her.

Elizabeth faltered then stopped, tears running down her cheeks.

Chapter 5

Michael worked his anger out on the road. He was digging, and with every stroke of the spade his rage faded slightly. His brothers Niall and Liam were with him; they told him to slow down, because with the hunger they did not have the energy to keep up, but he ignored them.

At the end of the day, Fraser stood beside the Poor Law clerks as they handed the meal out.

He told every man that, unless the rent was paid in full, on time, they would be evicted.

Michael walked home, his hands in his pockets. In the field by the cottage, the oats were nearly ready for harvesting. If he sold them all, there would be enough to pay the rent, just about.

His mother made porridge with the meal, flavoured with wild garlic and an onion. Michael watched his brothers and sisters eat. He was not hungry. When his mother saw that he was not eating, she asked him if anything was wrong. Mechanically, he smiled, said he was fine and finished the food on his plate.

After the meal was over, he walked out into the evening. The air was soft, the sun was setting far to the west, casting long shadows over the land. Michael loved the land, especially at dusk, when the colours were muted. There was a magic about Ireland which he felt in his bones. His people had lived here since the beginning of time, long before the Roscawls had come over with Henry's invading armies.

The fever was gone now, but ten people had died, there were ten new graves in the graveyard beside the village church.

He felt a pang of pain when he thought about Elizabeth. He had not meant to hurt her, he had meant to thank her, to tell her how much she was helping. But his pride had surged, made him strike out in anger, not anger at what she had done but anger at the unfairness of his predicament. If he could take back the words, he would.

The image of her face, puzzled, hurt, floated before him. He blinked it away. His anger soared again, anger at the world that condemned him to a life of struggle. He had two strong arms, a good mind; he could make a living for himself, he knew that. But there was no living to be had within many miles of his home, only the struggle to survive the hunger. In Liverpool or Glasgow, he could get work. Railway labourers earned ten shillings a week, he had heard, but he did not have the fare to get there.

When Michael's father had been on his deathbed, he had called Michael to him. "Michael," he had said, "promise me. You'll take care of your mother and the wains."

Michael had promised, of course. He would have taken care of them anyway, it was his duty as his father's first born son.

He reached the river. He lay down on the bank, rolled up his sleeves and dropped his arms into the water His thoughts drifted with the flow of the water. If he had taken the locket from Elizabeth, there would have been money to pay his fare to Liverpool or Glasgow even after the rent was paid.

He was wondering if he dared risk taking his fare from the money he would get if he sold the oats; he could then pay the rent out of the money he earned.

All he wanted was a chance.

In the dining-room at the castle, Elizabeth put her spoon down. Usually, she liked lemon flummery, but she had no appetite. Michael's harsh words still echoed inside her head; she was feeling hurt and bruised. When she got home, she had cried herself to sleep; when morning came, she still felt very sad.

She looked at her parents. Her father was eating heartily, as always, her mother was just picking at her food. She waited until they had finished before she asked to be excused. Her mother nodded her permission. Elizabeth got up and went to the door, which the butler opened for her.

"Elizabeth seems subdued," she heard her father say, as the butler closed the door behind her. Elizabeth stopped, leaned closer to listen.

"I didn't notice," her mother replied.

"I suppose she must be missing Sarah," her father said.

"I'm going to take her to London with me next month. It's about time we thought about her marriage. The Cavendish boy, you know, the Duke's second son, he seems a good prospect."

Elizabeth winced. She had met Edward Cavendish at Sarah's wedding; he was rake thin and he had no chin.

"Boy seems like a bit of a weakling to me," Lord Roscawl said.

"He comes from an excellent family. I've talked to the Duchess. It would be a good match. You know, Elizabeth's got to grow up sometime. She spends too much time on her own. She's running wild, I fear."

"It's something to think about," her father said. She heard the sound of his chair scraping against the floor as he got up.

Quaking inside, Elizabeth walked to her room. She could not bear the thought of marriage to Edward Cavendish, or to any of the other young men she knew. I'm too young, she thought, and then remembered that Sarah had become betrothed at the age that she was now. In society, it was expected that women were married in their late teens; a woman of twenty who was not married was considered an old maid.

She threw herself down on her bed and sobbed. Michael's face swam before her eyes, blurred by tears. It was him that she loved, she realized then. She cursed the unfairness of a world that would not let her choose her own husband, that condemned him to a life of penury whilst she lived in splendour at the castle.

His angry words rang in her ears. She did not know why he had been so enraged; she had only been trying to help. He had told her that he needed to pay the rent, and the only thing she could do was to give him the locket.

What was wrong with that?

For a long time, Elizabeth wondered, and then she remembered something that Nanny O'Dwyer had said. "We're proud, us Irish," the old lady had told her. "Though it's a sin, we can't help it. Sometimes, our pride is the only thing we have."

Suddenly, Elizabeth realized what she had done to Michael. By trying to give him the locket, she had injured his pride.

She went to the window and looked out at the land, fragile in the light of the moon. There had to be a way of helping without him knowing about it. Whatever it was, she would find it and she would do it.

After a long time, she washed the tears from her eyes, then she went to bed. Elizabeth was strong, despite her pampered upbringing. No matter what her parents wanted her to do, she would not marry Edward Cavendish, or anyone else that they chose for her. Somehow, she would find a way to salve the hurt she had inflicted upon Michael's pride.

In the morning, she rode out alone, over the hills. Passing the village of Roscawl, she rode on to the next village, where the priest lived. There, she knocked on the door of the priest's house and waited for an answer.

The old priest opened the door, peering at her through faded blue eyes shadowed by cataracts. "Why, come in, dear," he said. "Aren't you the young lady Roscawl?"

"Yes, Father," she said. She had never spoken to the priest before, although she had seen him in the village when she passed through. The Roscawls were Episcopalians, they worshipped in the Church of Ireland chapel in the castle grounds.

"Take a seat, my girl, and I'll put the kettle on and we'll have a cup of tea."

Elizabeth sat down on a wooden chair by the fire as the priest made tea.

"Now, young lady," he said, once he had served it, "what can I do for you?"

The tea was bitter, there was no milk or sugar. Elizabeth drank it for politeness' sake. She handed him the two shillings from her father and her gold locket. "I'd like you to sell this, Father, and put the money towards paying the rents in Roscawl."

The locket glinted in the light of the fire as the priest peered at it. "What a fine thing it is," he said.

"I would give you the money," Elizabeth said, "but I have none."

"Now isn't that a thing," he said, smiling, "the young lady from the castle saying she has no money."

"I don't," she said quickly. "I've asked my father. He only gave me two shillings."

He looked at her in a kindly way. "I wasn't criticizing you, young lady. It's a very kind thing that you are doing."

The light in the cottage was very dim. Elizabeth's eyes adjusted slowly; she saw how thin the priest was, how the folds of his cassock flapped about his spindly legs.

"I wish I could do more…" Her voice tailed off helplessly. She would give everything she had to lift the burden from Michael's shoulders. She knew that he was ashamed of his need; he had no need to be, she thought no less of him for it.

"Once I sell this, I'll be able to pay the rent of the whole village, I should think."

Elizabeth smiled and thanked him; he said, she should not be thanking him, he was the one who had to thank her.

"It's you that's been leaving the food," he said, as she rose to leave.

She nodded.

"Bless you, child."

"Father, I'm sorry, I would've left food before, but I didn't know. It was only this summer that I realized how bad things were."

He smiled sadly, waved to her as she rode away.

On the way back to the castle, Elizabeth decided to talk to her father again. Although she was not close to her parents – like all the children of the aristocracy, she had been brought up by her nanny and then a governess – she sensed that he was a good man, that he would not let people starve. He had always been kind to her; if she needed anything, he made sure that she had it.

The rent the villagers paid was very little, really. It would not cost him much to waive it until the potatoes started to grow again.

In the stables, she handed her horse over to Jamie, then she walked into the castle, along the corridor to her father's study. As she leaned towards the door to knock, she heard voices coming from inside.

"I've thought about it," her father was saying. "It would cost thousands of pounds to pay their fare to America. I just can't afford it, not with the rates rising the way they are."

"You don't have to pay their fare to America," Fraser said.

"You can't just turf them out, man."

"Why not? They've had plenty of chances. Most of them

haven't paid a penny rent for two years now, some of them three. Best be rid of the lot of them, Milord. They're nothing but a nuisance, anyway. The land would be better under sheep."

"Where would they go?"

"The Poorhouse in Kilkenny, I suppose. They'd be fed there. You're paying for it already, you know, with your rates."

"I don't like the idea of it."

"Milord, you can't have tenants who don't pay their rent. You can't let them get away with it for another year. If you did, even if the potatoes start growing again, you'd not get a penny piece out of them."

"I'll think about it," her father said.

"Milord, if you forgive me, that's what you said last time. I need a decision."

"I'll let you know next week," her father said.

Elizabeth shrank back into the shadows as the factor came out of her father's study. She waited a moment, then knocked and went in. Her father was poring over some figures in a ledger. His face broke into a smile when he saw her.

"Elizabeth! My dear, how are you?"

She tried to smile, but she was too worried to smile properly. "I couldn't help overhearing," she began. "Father, you're not going to evict the tenants, are you?"

He frowned, closed the ledger. "It's nothing for you to worry your pretty little head about, my dear."

"But you won't, will you?"

He folded his hands on top of the ledger. "In many ways, it would be the kindest thing to do."

Elizabeth stared at him.

"You see, the smallholdings they have, they will never support anything but the most meagre of livelihoods. If they were somewhere else, they would have the chance to improve themselves. If they stay here, they will always be dirt poor."

"But you said you won't send them to America."

"Elizabeth, I got an estimate from a shipping agent in Cork. It would cost more than five thousand pounds to send them to America. Do you have any idea of how much money that is? Apart from anything else, they've cost me a fortune already, between what I've paid in rates and what I could have got if I'd put the land under sheep years ago."

"I don't have to go to London," she said. "You could save that money, and use it for them."

"Don't be ridiculous, Elizabeth. You're the daughter of a lord. You have to take your rightful place in society. Now, I wish you'd listen to me. Don't you worry about the tenants. Let me do that. You just concentrate on enjoying yourself."

Elizabeth sensed that he would not listen if she said anything else, so she got up and went away. She realized that the locket she had given the priest would do no good. Although it might pay this year's rent, it would not be enough to pay the arrears that Fraser was determined to collect.

With Michael's angry words still ringing in her ears, she went upstairs to her room, threw herself down on her bed, and burst into tears.

Chapter 6

As Michael worked through the week, his anger faded and turned into pain. He had not meant to hurt Elizabeth, it had been an impulse, but because he had hurt her, he had also hurt himself. He wondered how he could say sorry.

Some tinkers passed through Roscawl, his mother swapped one of her pans for some pickling salt and she salted the fish that he caught for the winter.

Michael decided to sell the oats and pay the rent; if they had a roof over their heads they could manage, somehow, on the meagre meal rations from the roadworks and the fish that he poached. Then Fraser said it was not enough to pay that year's rent, to avoid eviction he had to pay the arrears as well.

Michael realized that he was trapped then, there was no way that he could raise the money he needed.

"Don't worry," his mother said, "you know we can go and stay with your uncle in Cork."

But he saw the look in her eyes, the hard lines etched into the skin of her face.

That night, after Fraser had given his edict, the young men of the village gathered outside.

"We'll fight," one said.

"With what?" Michael asked. "Sticks and stones?"

"What do you suggest, then?"

Michael thought a moment. "We won't move. We'll link arms and stand firm. There's more of us than there is of them."

"Aye, but they've the power. They've the guns. They'll drive us out somehow. They'll find a way."

Michael thought fleetingly that they could take the castle, that it was unguarded, that they could invade it the way Roscawl's ancestors had invaded their land hundreds of years ago. But if they did that, he realized, the wrath of the landlords would be terrible. All the soldiers in Ireland would be called to drive them out. The bloodshed would be great; in the end, they would not win.

What would be the point?

There was an old man among them who remembered the rising of '98, fifty years before. "You can't fight 'em," he said, his old eyes rheumy and sad. "They'd only kill you all."

Michael thought that, if there was any justice in the world, then the time would come when the Irish would be able to drive the English and the landlords out of their land. The meeting broke up and the men drifted home, a sense of despondency heavy on their shoulders.

He would have to find a way to contact Elizabeth, to say goodbye to her and thank her for what she had done. Although he hated the landlords, he did not, could not, hate Elizabeth. She was different. He had to apologize to her for what he had said.

The next day, Michael went to the priest's house after he had worked on the road, and asked if he could borrow a pen and have a bit of paper. The priest gave him what he asked for, and let him sit at the table to write his letter.

Dear Elizabeth, Michael wrote.
I am sorry about the things I said to you. I did not mean them; I was not angry at you, I am just angry at the way things are. You have helped us a lot, and I am very grateful to you. I hope that we can still be friends. I will be at the river every night, if you would like to come to talk to me. I hope you do.
Your friend, Michael.

He blotted the letter carefully, then folded it and put it into his pocket. He was glad then that he had learned to write at the village school. He thanked the priest, then left.

At school, Michael had been clever. The teacher told him that he could study for the priesthood, if he liked; the priesthood was the only occupation open to a young Irish Catholic boy. Although Michael had been flattered, he refused because he did not have a vocation. He wanted to learn about the world, to use his brain to make a better living for himself and his family. As he walked home, he smiled bitterly to himself.

The only free time he had was on Sunday; there was no work on the road then. After church, he walked to the castle and hesitantly knocked at the kitchen door. After a long time, Mrs Murphy, the cook opened it. She glared at him. Mrs Murphy had firm ideas about the world; people had their place, she thought, and a boy like Michael was not to come knocking at the castle door.

"There's no work", she said, "if that's what you're wanting."

"I didn't come for work," Michael said quickly.

"What did you come for, then?"

He handed her the letter. "Will you give this to Miss Elizabeth, please?"

She stared at it, then at him; grudgingly, she nodded.

Michael thanked her, then he turned to walk away.

The kitchen was empty. Lunch was over; the roast for dinner was cooking slowly in the oven. Mrs Murphy looked at the paper in her hand, then she unfolded it. The words meant nothing to her, she had never learned to read, she had never needed to. She did not know what the letter was, but she did not think any good would come of it. A boy from the village had no reason to write to the daughter of the castle. The letter was probably a plea for more food or money, yet Elizabeth had already done all she could. It was not fair to ask her to do any more, Mrs Murphy thought, but she knew that if Elizabeth read the letter, she would feel bad.

She thought for a time, then threw the letter on to the kitchen fire and watched the flames eat up the paper.

That was the right thing to do, she thought. If Lord Roscawl knew that a lad from the village had been writing to his daughter, he would be furious.

Mrs Murphy had a soft spot for Elizabeth; she did not want her to get hurt.

Michael waited at the river every day for a week, but Elizabeth did not come. He thought that she had become bitter, that he had hurt her too much. He was annoyed with himself, also saddened. He had thought that when she got his letter, she would be sure to come.

Fraser had started the gamekeepers patrolling the river, to stop the villagers from poaching fish. He wondered if that was it, if she was scared of being seen with him. The gamekeepers did not worry Michael; they were Irish too and they would not do much if they caught him. They would just clip his ear and take away the fish he'd caught, and he could tolerate that.

He was afraid that Elizabeth would stop bringing food as well, but when he walked home in the middle of the week, he saw that she had been round again and left a parcel at every cottage.

He realized that she did not hate him then.

The dressmaker came from Cork. Although the dressmakers in London were more fashionable, Lady Roscawl said that Elizabeth needed a new outfit to travel in, she could not wait until she got there. She did not notice the pain etched deeply upon her daughter's face.

Elizabeth stood meekly in her petticoats while the dressmaker measured her and noted the figures.

"How much will this cost?" she asked as the woman worked, once her mother had left the room.

"Tsk, Miss Elizabeth, I'm not sure now, but it won't be much, it won't be nearly as much as they're charging in London."

"How much?" Elizabeth insisted.

"Well, I'm not sure, it depends exactly how much cloth I need, but I think thirty shillings or so, in this blue velvet.

It's a beautiful colour, Miss, it brings out the blue of your eyes."

Elizabeth looked thoughtful.

"Is there anything the matter, Miss?" the dressmaker asked her. "My prices are keen, so they are."

"It's just that a whole family could live for a year on that," Elizabeth said.

"Well, yes," the dressmaker said, "I suppose they could, but I wouldn't worry about it, Miss. Just thank the Lord for how lucky you are."

Elizabeth waited anxiously until the dressmaker finished, then she rushed down the stairs to the corridor outside her father's office. She had been watching for the factor all week and from her bedroom window she had seen him arrive.

Through the door, she listened as he gave her father a summary of the workings of the estate. Wheat in particular had been doing well, Fraser said; there would be a bumper harvest.

"I've given a lot of thought to what you said about the tenants," her father said. "I've decided that, if they can make even some small contribution to the arrears, I will not evict them. It would be inhumane to drive them out."

Elizabeth sighed with relief. With the money from her locket, there would be just enough, Michael and the others would not be evicted. Despite the way he had hurt her, she still cared for him, she could not help it.

Fraser coughed. "I beg to differ, Milord. There's lawlessness about. The Young Irelanders are on the rampage. There'll be trouble, mark my words."

"I don't think so," her father said. "We've never had any

trouble here. Besides, the government's got precautions well in hand."

Elizabeth slipped away, happy for a moment. I'll have to tell Michael, she thought, then she remembered his angry words, and the pain came back.

That night, at dinner, her mother said that they would leave for London next week. Her father frowned, said that there was trouble in Dublin, maybe she would be better to wait until William and Albert, Elizabeth's brothers, were home from Oxford.

"Trouble," Lady Roscawl said angrily, "what trouble?"

"There's a rabble on the loose. There's been talk of trouble ever since that fellow Mitchel was deported. Nothing to worry about, my dear, but I'd rather you stick to safety until it's all over."

Elizabeth breathed a sigh of relief.

"That's very inconvenient," her mother said.

"Maybe, but better safe than sorry."

"I've already written to say we'll be coming."

"Don't worry, my dear; if the worst comes to the worst I'll ask the garrison to give you an escort." Lord Roscawl turned to his daughter. "I've been meaning to say to you, Elizabeth, don't ride out beyond the home farm. There's a lot of talk going on, and I don't want you to take any risks."

"Yes," she said, meekly.

Chapter 7

Elizabeth's brothers came home a week later. William, the eldest, was Lord Roscawl's heir; he spent most of the time closeted with his father in the study. He bore his responsibilities gravely; he had no time for his sister. Albert did, though. They rode out together around the boundaries of the home farm.

"How are you?" he asked her, after a while.

Elizabeth shrugged. "Mother wants to marry me off to Edward Cavendish."

Albert laughed. "Don't you want to marry him?"

"Would you?"

Albert gazed at her. "You'll have to get married sometime."

Elizabeth shivered. "Not yet. And not to Edward Cavendish." Albert was lucky, she thought. He was a boy, a man, and because he was not the heir nobody expected anything of him. There was talk of him buying a commission, joining the army and maybe going off to the colonies. He could do anything he wanted with his life.

"What's going on?" she asked him.

"You mean, in England?"

She nodded.

"There's been revolutions all over – in Prussia, Austria,

Venice, Milan. There's talk of revolution here."

"In Ireland?"

"Yes, but it won't come to anything. Dublin's full of troops. There's more troops than there are people. It's O'Brien Smith's mob that's causing problems, you know."

Elizabeth did not know.

"The Young Irelanders, they call themselves. They were tried for treasonable felony a couple of months ago. O'Brien Smith and Meagher got off, Mitchel was deported. That pair of rascals have been trying to talk up a rebellion ever since. But the people are too hungry to fight. All their energy goes digging roads."

"It isn't fair," Elizabeth said.

"What isn't?"

"The potatoes. There's other food, there's grain and there's meat. Nobody should have to go hungry."

Albert shrugged. "There's too many people in Ireland. Even before the blight, they could hardly feed themselves."

"Yes, but it isn't fair."

"I don't understand you, Elizabeth."

"It's not fair that we should have so much, and they have nothing."

Albert laughed. "Now you're talking like a rebel."

"You know what I mean. The tenants have been here forever. They've paid rent for hundreds of years. They have a right to our help when times are hard."

The sunlight was strong. Albert raised his hand to shield his eyes as he looked at her. "We are helping, Elizabeth. There's no need for anyone to go hungry. There's work on the road…"

"Not everybody can work on the road, Albert."

"No, but men with a family to support get extra. There's enough food to go around, Elizabeth. Really, there is. It's costing Pater a fortune. He was saying this morning that the rates are twenty times what they were three years ago. And I don't think he's seen a penny rent from the small tenants in that time."

"Albert, there isn't enough food. People are so hungry that they're going down with fever, and they're dying from it."

He shook his head. "That's not true. It's rebel propaganda."

"It is true. I've seen it with my own eyes."

He stared at her. "What?"

Elizabeth took a deep breath. "I've been going to the village for a while now. I take food, some meal and whatever's spare from the kitchen."

"You'll get into dreadful trouble if you get caught."

"Yes, but you see, Fraser's in charge of the roadworks, and you know what he's like. If he doesn't like someone's face, then they don't get work. He's not giving out all the meal like he's supposed to. He's been selling some of it to the merchants in Cork."

Albert fell silent, avoiding her eyes as he stared at the horizon.

"Are you sure?" he asked her, after a while.

"Pretty sure."

"Have you told Pater?"

"I tried to, but I don't have proof. Father said it was just a vicious slander."

"Well, that's what it probably is. You know, Lizibeth, there's a lot of hot talk going around, with the rebels.

They're trying to stir up trouble everywhere. I doubt Fraser would risk his job by doing something like that."

"Albert, can you talk to Father?"

He smiled sadly. "What could I say? If there's no proof, there's no proof."

"Will you at least help me take food to the village?"

Albert spoke very slowly. "Lizibeth, I'd rather not. Heaven knows what Pater would do if he found out. It's different for you. You're a girl, and he's always had a soft spot for you."

"Don't you care, Albert?"

Again, he avoided her eyes. "Of course I do, Lizibeth. It's just that I have to be careful, you know, not being the heir. It wouldn't do to get Pater mad at me."

They rode home in silence. Elizabeth was bitterly disappointed; she had hoped that Albert would understand, that he would help her with her meagre efforts to feed the tenants. But he was more concerned for himself than he was for them. Oxford had changed him, she thought, but not for the better.

At dinner, Lady Roscawl announced that she and Elizabeth would leave for London on Monday of the following week. Elizabeth stiffened, but said nothing. Her father said that he would send a message to the garrison at Kilkenny and arrange an escort for them.

"We had no trouble, Father," William said.

"Maybe so, but it's better to be safe than sorry," her father replied.

After dinner, Elizabeth was supposed to make small talk with her mother in the drawing-room while her father and brothers drank port and smoked cigars. She found herself at a loss for something to say.

"You're very lucky, you know," her mother said. "The Cavendish boy is an excellent match. Even though he's the younger son, there's plenty of money. They have a beautiful house in London, you won't be stuck in this God forsaken island all the time. And the brother, the heir, his wife hasn't produced a son yet. There might be a problem. You could be the mother of a duke."

Elizabeth shivered inwardly.

"Well, dear, what do you say?"

"I ... I don't love him, Mother," she blurted.

"Tush, girl, what's love? It's a very good match. You have to take your place in society."

"But I'd rather wait. Surely I don't have to get married for a year or two yet?"

"Talk like that, my girl, and you'll end up a spinster. And you don't want that, do you?"

Elizabeth thought that she would rather be a spinster than the wife of Edward Cavendish. She did not say so, though, and her mother took her silence for assent.

"You see? Your father and I want to do the right thing for you, Elizabeth. You don't have to worry. We'll take care of your interests."

Elizabeth nodded glumly, thinking that was what she was afraid of. It was not that she disliked or disrespected her parents, it was just that they were so distant from her that she hardly knew them. She doubted that love had come into their marriage; it was, she supposed, a "good" match for the youngest daughter of a baronet with limited assets. Yet she had read *Wuthering Heights* surreptitiously when it appeared in the library along the corridor, and she had sensed something of the emotion that had played so little part in her life so far. She knew that, in the novel, Catherine regretted to the end of her life the snobbery that had cost her the chance of marriage to Heathcliff. Elizabeth did not want to make the same mistake. Sometimes, she wished that she could be more like her sister Sarah, that she could fill her mind with thoughts of what clothes to wear, that she could marry happily the man her parents chose for her.

Finally, her mother rang for her maid, said that it was time to retire. Elizabeth said good night and went up to her own room.

Eithne looked at her closely as she brushed her hair. "Are you all right, Miss Elizabeth? You look powerfully peaky."

Elizabeth smiled sadly. "I'm fine, Eithne."

"You're as white as a sheet."

"My parents want me to marry Edward Cavendish," Elizabeth blurted.

"And what's the matter with that?"

"I don't love him, Eithne. I'll never love him. I don't even like him. I can't bear the thought of spending my life with him."

Eithne gazed at her; Elizabeth suddenly realized how flippant her concerns were, when Eithne was worried about keeping her family alive.

"I'm sorry," she said. "I'm just being selfish."

"You are not, Miss Elizabeth. I'd be powerfully angry if someone tried to marry me off to a man I didn't want."

The soft strokes of the brush through her hair soothed

Elizabeth. "I would have to leave here, I'd have to live in London," she said. "I don't ever want to leave Ireland."

Eithne shook her head. "You know, your – let me see – great-grandmother, she was Irish, she was one of us. She was a village girl and she married the lord. A good woman, she was, a good wife and good to her people. You know, you take after her, they say."

"I didn't know that," Elizabeth said slowly.

"Och, yes, Miss. Her name was Grainne; she was fair like you, with blue eyes too."

"My parents never told me. They never talk about her."

Eithne shrugged. "Maybe they're ashamed. Maybe they think the lord had no place marrying a village girl. But you know what they say. Blood will out."

"But why ... I mean, we're related to you, aren't we? We're related to the village people?"

"There's a lot of water under the bridge since then, Miss Elizabeth. In the '98 rising, some men from the village went. The lord never forgave them. That would be – let me see – your grandfather. Grainne's son. Half Irish, he was, yet he sided with the English. Grainne was dead by then. She's buried in the graveyard outside the chapel. You can go to see her grave anytime."

Eithne finished brushing her hair, Elizabeth thanked her. She undressed, then she went to bed, but she did not sleep. She lay awake thinking about her great-grandmother, Grainne, and the Irish blood that ran in her veins.

Michael went to early Mass on Sunday. Two weeks had passed since he had sent his note to Elizabeth, and he still had not heard from her. She still brought food though, twice a week. He had not seen her, he had been too busy poaching trout, but the salt was finished now, his mother was smoking the fish he caught above the fire. One of the gamekeepers had almost caught him, he had come round to the cottage to give him a warning, but Michael was not bothered. There were plenty of places on the river where he could catch fish; the gamekeepers could not watch all of them.

Elizabeth was still on his mind all of the time; he was so sure that she would come to see him, that she would forgive him. He wondered what was keeping her back.

When the service was over, he saw the castle maids leaving the tiny church. On impulse, he ran after them.

"Which one of you works for Elizabeth?" he asked.

Eithne looked at him. "I work for Miss Elizabeth," she said. "What do you want with her?"

Michael hesitated. "It's just that I sent her a note," he said, after a moment. "To thank her for the food she gives us. I wonder if she got it."

"I'm sure she did," Eithne said.

"Can you ask her? Just to make sure?"

"I suppose I can."

Michael thanked her, and walked back to his cottage. Now that he was sure that the village was facing eviction, he had decided to use the money he would get from selling the oats to pay his fare to Liverpool. Once there, he would find work and send the money home to feed his family. Although he did not want to leave them, he had no choice, really. It was Liverpool or the poor house. But he wanted to make his peace with Elizabeth before he left.

Chapter 8

Elizabeth's trunk was packed, her new travelling suit hanging in her wardrobe. She did not want to go, but she had no choice – her mother was determined to take her. She consoled herself with the thought that Cook had promised to send food to the village; that every week, Jamie would take some meal. She was not going to London for ever, just for a month.

As Eithne brushed her hair before she went to bed, she pursed her lips and said, "I hope you don't think I'm being forward, Miss Elizabeth, but a lad from the village, Michael, he asked me if you got the letter he sent."

Elizabeth's heart skipped a beat. "What letter?"

"I don't know, Miss. He just said he'd sent you a letter."

"I didn't get any letter, Eithne. What did it say?"

"I don't know, Miss."

Impatiently, Elizabeth waited for the maid to finish with her hair. She went to bed and then, when the castle was silent, she got up, dressed, and went out. In the stables, she saddled her horse herself, then led it out into the yard and through the gate. Once she was on the track, she mounted the horse and set off for the village. She was not sure where Michael would be so she decided to try down by the river first. She found him at a pool about a mile beyond Roscawl.

"Hello," she said, shyly.

He got up, shook the water from his hands. "Hello, Elizabeth. You got my letter, then?"

"No. What did it say?"

"Ach." He looked away, embarrassed. "I left it with the cook."

Elizabeth thought. Mrs Murphy could be funny sometimes. "She didn't give it to me. What did it say, Michael?"

"Ach," he said again, "just that I was sorry, you know. I didn't mean to be nasty to you, that night you tried to give me your locket. I was angry."

"Why were you angry? Were you angry at me?"

"No," he said quickly. "It's just this damned potato blight. I don't want you to be giving me things, Elizabeth." He was going to say that he wanted to be the one who gave things to her, but he did not. He knew that he would have sounded stupid. What would a lad like him ever have to give a girl like her?

Elizabeth smiled at him. She got off her horse. "There isn't much I can do," she said. "I never liked the locket anyway."

They began to walk back towards the village.

"I'm going away," he said.

Elizabeth's heart lurched.

"We're going to be evicted…"

"No, you aren't," she cut in. "I heard Father talking about it. He's told Fraser not to evict you." She did not tell him that she had given the locket to the priest to pay the rent.

He stopped, looked at her. "Is that right?"

"It is, Michael."

"Well, Fraser's still threatening us."

"He'll stop," she said, assuredly.

Michael thought for a moment. If there was no risk of eviction, then he could stay in Roscawl. He was happy for an instant until he realized that he should still go away, that the only way out of the vicious circle of poverty for his family was if he went away to find work.

He swore softly under his breath. "I still have to go away," he told Elizabeth.

She looked at him; she looked so beautiful in the moonlight that his heart ached.

"I have to go away to find work. Liverpool, most likely. If I get work on the railways, then I can feed my folks and pay the rent as well."

Elizabeth's heart lurched again. She wondered if she could say anything to change his mind, thought that she could not. Work was what he needed, and she could never offer him that.

"When are you going?"

"September, most likely. When I'm sure we won't be evicted. I'll use the money from the oats to pay my fare."

September was only six weeks away, and for four of them Elizabeth would be in London. Haltingly, she told him that, but told him not to worry about the meal, because Jamie would give it out.

He touched her hand briefly. "Do you have to go?"

She thought, it was not fair, she should not have to. "Yes," she said. She felt a thrill when he touched her, as if a bolt of lightning had shot through her. "But I'll be back. You won't be gone until after I'm back."

"I suppose not."

"And you won't stay in Liverpool for ever, will you?"

"I don't know, I don't think so." He thought of telling her about his dreams of America, decided not to for fear that he would sound foolish.

"I'll miss you, Michael."

"I'll miss you, Elizabeth."

They had reached the village; the cottages rose darkly against the night.

"When the blight's over," he began, then he stopped.

"What, Michael?"

"Ach." He looked away from her. "I was going to say that I'll come back when the blight's over, but you'll be wed, by then."

"No," she said, sharply.

"Yes, you will. You'll meet some fine young lord and wed him."

"No, I won't," she said.

"See," he said, "when the blight's over, my brothers, they'll be grown. I've always thought I'd head for America, try to make my fortune." He stopped talking abruptly, realized that he had told her, when he had not meant to.

She was smiling at him, the light of the moon in her eyes.

"Ach." He shook his head. "I'm just a daft dreamer, so I am."

"You are not daft, Michael. Whatever you are, you aren't that."

"So we'll meet again, in a few weeks' time?"

"Yes," she said.

Elizabeth rode home slowly. She was not aware of the

horse's movements, she felt as if she was floating on air. She relived the thrill she had felt when he touched her; he still likes me, she thought. By instinct, though, she knew that it was more than that; he felt the same attraction for her that she felt for him. How strange it is, she thought, this feeling that she had for him. They had known each other most of their lives, he had always been her friend but now she wanted him to be more than that.

Elizabeth did not care for the wealth that surrounded her in the castle; she did not care for her station in life as the daughter of a lord. What she cared for was Ireland: she wanted to be free to live her life there, with Michael in the land that she loved.

Although she did not want to go to London, she thought that if she went there, she might find some way of getting some money. Maybe her mother would give her a piece of jewellery that she could sell, or she could some-how lay her hands on the money that her mother intended to spend on clothes for her. She had been to London before, her father owned a house on the lane overlooking the park, but she did not like it. She missed the open spaces of Ireland, the hills and the wide, wide sky. What-ever anyone said, she was Irish, she had been born there and the land was in her blood.

It would be easy to thwart her mother's plan to marry her off to Edward Cavendish; all she had to do was to be rude to him, or, better still, his mother. In the clannish London society, the Irish aristocracy was considered un-couth anyway.

She reached the castle, went to bed, fell asleep instantly with a smile on her face.

Eithne woke her with tea in the morning. It was a beautiful day, the sun was streaming in through the window.

Elizabeth drank her tea quickly, then dressed in her new travelling dress and cape. Eithne was not coming with her, her mother's maid was accompanying them on the journey, and there were plenty of servants in the London house.

At breakfast, her father and brothers talked about the coming shooting season; as always, Lord Roscawl would host a house party.

The coach was waiting in the stable yard. Lady Roscawl got in first, then Elizabeth and Brigid, her mother's maid. The garrison commander had sent three soldiers to accompany them.

They set off, the hooves of the soldiers' horses throwing up sparks from the cobbles of the yard. Elizabeth swayed with the motion of the coach, yawned. The journey to Dublin would take all of the day, they would spend the night there, with friends of her mother, then leave on the boat to England the next morning.

The windows of the coach were small; Elizabeth could not see much through them. After a while, she opened the book she had brought with her to read, a copy of *Jane Eyre* that she had taken from the library.

Lady Roscawl stared at it balefully. "I found it tiresome," she said. "The heroine has little to recommend herself."

Elizabeth smiled politely, tried to read but the print jumped so much with the movement that after a while she gave up and closed the book. Usually, she liked novels, she enjoyed the opportunity of learning how other people lived their lives. Her own life at the castle was very narrow; beyond what she knew of people in the village she had little knowledge of the world beyond its boundaries. She had read the novels of Jane Austen, had perceived some parallels between her life and the lives of Austen's heroines, though they had much more freedom than she did, she thought.

A woman's role was to grow up and make a good marriage – she had known that all of her life. Sometimes – often – she envied her brothers for the freedom they had to go out into the world and learn about it. It was not fair that men could do so much and women could do so little. Although she enjoyed learning, her education had been abruptly terminated last year, when she was deemed to have a passable knowledge of English and Latin, music and art. It was inconceivable that she could learn beyond the elements of what she needed to make polite conversation. A university education was unthinkable for a woman; her brothers complained about the onerous studying, but she would have loved the chance they had.

Lord Roscawl had banned the works of Charles Dickens from the library. The man was scurrilous, he said, but Elizabeth, who had read about the author in *The Times*, had borrowed a copy of *Oliver Twist* from Albert and read it secretly. The novel shocked her, she was appalled that people had to live like that. The real crime was poverty, she thought. It was unfair that children had to beg and steal in order to survive. Albert said that she did not understand the world; some people were rich and some were poor. That was that, he said.

They were lucky to be rich.

The window of the coach had fogged with condensation. Elizabeth wiped it with her hand and watched the rich fields rolling past. There was wheat growing in some fields, cows grazing in other ones. Ireland produced plenty of food; it was a crime that people were being allowed to starve.

The work of Dickens had been a revelation to her; after she had finished *Oliver Twist*, she knew that she was not alone in the world, that other people thought as she did. It would be easy for her father, the lord, to share a little of his wealth. She did not need all the dresses that she had, her mother did not need all her jewellery. Most of the food that was served at the table was never eaten, it could so easily be shared out amongst the hungry villagers. Her father certainly did not need the meagre rents they paid. The estate produced enough in grain and cattle and rents from the big farms to keep them in comfort. Elizabeth felt her anger rise at her father's selfishness. Yet he was her father, he loved her in his way and she supposed that she loved him.

She understood Michael's anger better now, once she had thought about it.

The coach jolted to a halt, disturbing her reverie. She looked out, saw one of the soldiers talking to another one. Her mother had been dozing; she jerked awake and asked what the matter was.

Elizabeth did not know. She opened the door of the coach and called to the young lieutenant who was leading her escort.

He smiled at her, saluted smartly. "No trouble, ma'am. It's just that there's a bit of a rabble in Kilkenny."

Lady Roscawl leaned forward. "What do you mean, a rabble?"

The lieutenant cleared his throat. "It's nothing to worry about, my lady. Just a gang of these ruffians, Young Irelanders, they call themselves."

Lady Roscawl flinched. "We'd best turn back, then."

"We could avoid them by going around the town."

"I don't want to take the risk," she said, firmly.

"Very well, my lady."

Elizabeth's spirits lifted at the knowledge that they would not be going to London, after all. She looked sharply at her mother, wondering at her sudden change of heart. Lady Roscawl had a look of triumph on her face.

They got back to the castle after lunchtime. Lady Roscawl called for tea and sandwiches; she ate, then told Elizabeth that she was going to see her father.

Elizabeth waited, then crept along the corridor to listen to what she was going to say.

"This country is pagan, heathen," Lady Roscawl said. "I mean, what kind of place is it when law-abiding people cannot travel safely for fear of running into a rabble somewhere? It really has gone too far, William."

Elizabeth's father cleared his throat. "What can I do, Margaret?"

"Well, for one thing, you can make sure that I can live in safety."

"You are perfectly safe here, Margaret."

"For how long? What happens when the rabble comes here?"

"You know that won't happen, Margaret," Lord Roscawl said, patiently. "The trouble's confined to the cities..."

"Ha! We were just outside Kilkenny! They're on the loose! They're everywhere!"

"You're exaggerating, Margaret. We've got precautions well in hand. There's more troops in Dublin than there's people, and habeas corpus is being suspended, so there's no problem about throwing the lot of them in jail."

"I don't like it, William. I just don't like it."

Elizabeth realized then why her mother had a look of triumph on her face when the soldier told her about the rabble; she wanted to leave Ireland for good and the rabble was an excellent excuse.

"What would you like me to do?"

"When it's safe to travel, I want to go to London. I want to stay there until all this trouble is over."

"Margaret…"

"I'm sick of it, William. I'm sick of being stuck here on my own, without any decent company. It's all right for you, you spend half of your time at the House of Lords. Do you ever think about me? What sort of a life is it here? I'm fed up with it. Truly, I am."

"All right," her father said tiredly. "You can stay in London."

"I don't understand," her mother said petulantly. "We could live quite happily in London. Elizabeth would be able to meet people, take her place in society. I don't know why you insist upon living here."

"You know the reason, Elizabeth."

"I do not."

"It's my land, woman. My birthright. I'm not going to give it up because some stupid rabble's on the loose. There's been trouble before, and we've always defeated them. This time will be no different."

"I prefer to spend my time in London, with decent people," her mother said coldly.

"Very well, Margaret," her father said. There was ice in his voice.

Elizabeth crept away, before her mother came out of the study. She realized something then, that her mother did not love her father, had probably never loved him. Lady Roscawl was a cold and distant figure to Elizabeth, she had never shown her any affection. Affection was something she had shown to none of her children; any comfort they'd had came from Nanny O'Dwyer.

For a moment, Elizabeth felt a shard of sympathy for her mother's loveless marriage; then she thought of her insensitivity and felt anger at her for her lack of compassion.

She did not know how long the trouble would last, but she had some time now. She had to find a way to avoid going to England; she could not stand it if she had to live there. She knew she could not talk to her father; she knew that he would say that her place was with her mother. Elizabeth wondered what she could do.

Chapter 9

With a heavy heart, Michael had watched the coach leaving as he worked on the road. Much later, he saw it coming back again; he wondered why. The Young Irelanders were on the march, he knew that, but they were no threat to anyone and certainly not to Lady Roscawl and her daughter. They were armed only with sticks, they did not have a gun between them. The rising would come to nothing. Michael suspected that many of the men who had joined had done so because they knew that it was a sure route to jail and that in jail they would surely be fed.

The most powerful force in Ireland that year was hunger.

The work on the road was tiring; Michael worked steadily but not hard. Through experience, he had learned to pace himself: the meagre rations of meal that he earned did not give him the energy to work hard.

At least, he thought, Elizabeth was not going to London, he would have the chance to talk to her again soon. The thought of her made him smile; the time that he spent with her was the only happiness he had in a life of unremitting drudgery. He sensed that she felt for him what he felt for her; although he knew that it was an impossible dream that they would ever be more than friends, he took comfort from the fact that she cared for him.

At the end of the week, he saw that the oats were ready for harvest. On Sunday, he reaped them with his brothers and sisters; they packed the oats into sacks ready to be sold.

"Will you sell them to O'Callaghan?" his mother asked him.

O'Callaghan was a gombeen-man, who worked in league with Fraser. Before the hunger he had lent money at exorbitant rates; when the hunger came, he bought produce for a pittance, knowing that the people had no choice but to sell to him. In the old days, he would organize boxing matches, paying the fighters pennies and making a fortune from the bets. He owned the inn in the village, which he had given up when he realized that nobody had any money to buy his ale any more. Michael hated him for making money from people's weaknesses.

"I'll be damned if I do," he replied, angrily.

His mother flinched, annoyed that he had sworn, but she said nothing about it. "What will you do, then?"

"I'll take the cart, sell it at the fair in Kilkenny. I'll get the best price there."

His mother looked at him. They had no horse; the horse they'd once owned had been sold to O'Callaghan to pay the rent three years ago, in the first year of the hunger. His father had wanted to sell the cart instead of the horse, but O'Callaghan said that carts were going begging all over the place.

"I can manage," Michael said. "I'll take Liam and Niall with me. We'll drag it ourselves."

"If you're sure," his mother said.

Michael had thought about it; going to the Kilkenny

fair was the only thing to do. The harvest had been good, he hoped that he could get thirty shillings for the oats, maybe more. Five shillings would take him to Liverpool; he would leave the rest of the money with his mother, to take care of her needs until he managed to send her money from his wages. If Elizabeth was right, there was no need to pay rent and even if she wasn't, they would have enough to pay it. Michael knew that he would earn enough from his wages to pay the arrears and to feed his family. For the first time that year, he felt hope for the future.

He talked to the other men in the village; nobody wanted to sell to O'Callaghan so they agreed that Michael and his brothers would take the oats to Kilkenny in two trips and they would share the meal that the other men earned on the road.

They set off very early on Monday morning, before the sun was up. The cart was stacked with sacks of oats, they tied ropes to the cart and dragged it. It was heavy work; they sang songs to keep their spirits up. Kilkenny was fifteen miles away; it would take most of the day to get there. Michael thought that, if they got enough for the oats, they could hire a horse for the second trip.

He breathed a sigh of relief when they passed the castle; he did not want Elizabeth to see him dragging the cart like a mule.

"You should let me go to England, Michael," Niall said. "I could stow away, no bother."

"You're too young," Michael said. Niall was only thirteen, he was still a boy.

"They'd never catch me," Niall said. He was a bit of a rogue.

"You know Mother wouldn't allow it, Niall."

They stopped for a rest once they reached the main road to Kilkenny. The town was only ten more miles away, they had come five miles in a couple of hours. Michael drank some water from a stream, then bound rags around his hands to try to keep the skin from blistering.

Niall was whistling a jaunty tune; Liam worked doggedly. "Once you're in England," he said to Michael, "will you send me the fare, let me come too?"

"Of course I will," Michael said.

"I'd like to earn a wage," Liam said. "A decent wage, not the rotten meal we get for working on the road."

They were maybe a mile down the road when they heard a loud crack; they turned round to see that the axle of the cart had snapped.

Michael swore; the axle was wood – it had rotted through.

"What do we do now, Michael?" Liam asked him.

Michael thought for a moment. Beyond the field, there was a wood; he told Niall to watch the cart while he and Liam went to find some bits of wood to fix the axle. He thought that if he could find a couple of pieces that were strong enough, he could brace them against the axle and bind them together with rope.

It took a long time to find the wood that he needed; he did not have an axe, so he had to whittle branches away with the little knife that he carried in his pocket to gut fish.

Once they got back to the cart, they unloaded the oats then Michael bound the pieces of wood to the axle with rope. It did not look too strong, but he hoped that it would hold. They had only gone a few yards when the axle tore apart again.

"What now, Michael?" Niall was looking at him as if he had the power to fix anything.

Michael was thinking that, if he had some decent wood, a hammer and some nails, he could fix the axle. But he had no wood, nor did he have a hammer and nails. His mother had sold their hammer to a gypsy when his father got the fever; in fact, she had exchanged it for some herbal brew that the gypsy said was good for fever.

He wondered if anyone in the village had a hammer; after three years of the hunger, he doubted it. Everything that was not absolutely necessary had been sold, long ago. He pondered for a moment, then realized that they were stuck.

"Go back to Roscawl," he told Niall. "Go to the men working on the road. See if anybody's got a hammer and nails, some strong wood to fix the axle. If they have, bring it back. If not, tell them what's happened. Tell them to come and help us carry the oats back. We can't manage them all ourselves."

Niall set off at a run. Michael and Liam sat down by the roadside.

Michael felt heartsick; he needed so much to be able to get to Kilkenny, to be able to get a decent price for his oats.

"We did our best," Liam said.

"Ach." Michael did not want to talk about it.

The sun was high in the sky; it would be several hours before Niall got back. Michael closed his eyes, began to doze.

Niall got back in the late afternoon. Nobody had a

hammer; he had told the men what had happened and they were coming to carry the oats back as soon as they finished at the road.

Michael saw the line of forlorn humanity a short while later, trudging along the road towards him. In silence, the men picked up a sack of oats each, slung it over their shoulders and began the long walk home.

"Don't fret," one of them said to Michael. "You did your best, son."

Once they had carried all the oats back, Michael left immediately with Liam to bring back the cart. Freed of the weight of the oats, the makeshift repair he had made to the axle held. By the time they reached Roscawl, the moon was high in the sky and they were exhausted.

The next day, old Joe Ryan looked at the axle. Michael's father had always owned the only cart in the village, but in the years before the hunger, Joe sometimes helped him keep it in good condition.

"Wood's rotted through, son," he said, picking at loose grains with his fingers. "Can't be repaired, so it can't. You'd need to replace it."

Michael sighed. That was what he had feared. He'd looked around, but there was no wood that he could replace the axle with, and even if he had the wood, he could not afford to pay the blacksmith to fit the wheels on.

O'Callaghan turned up that evening. He strutted into the village on a black horse, looking hale and hearty; most of all, fat. There were two men with him and another with a big cart.

Michael scowled at him; the gombeen-man's arrival was

greeted by a sullen silence.

"I hear the harvest's in," O'Callaghan said. "I've come to buy your oats."

Michael thought that he would rather the oats went to waste than he sold them to him. His mother had heard the horses; she came out of the cottage and told him, in a whisper, that O'Callaghan's money was as good as anyone else's.

"We'd be as well to keep them and eat them," he said to her.

"No. We need the money for your fare. We've food enough from the road, and the fish. We'll get by, Michael. The important thing is you getting to Liverpool, finding work."

Michael queued up with the other men. One by one, they sold their oats. When it came to Michael's turn, O'Callaghan looked at the sacks he had harvested, then at a list in his hand.

"I'll give you twenty-five shillings," he said.

"Come on, O'Callaghan, you know it's worth thirty, at least."

"Twenty-five shillings, take it or leave it."

Michael nodded, too angry to speak. The oats were loaded on to O'Callaghan's cart as he waited with the other men to be paid. When all the oats were loaded, O'Callaghan looked around at the men of the village, smirking.

"Our money," Michael said.

"Well, my young lad, I've done you a favour, me and my friend, Mr Fraser. He tells me the rent's not paid yet, so I'll save you the trouble and pay the money to him."

Michael felt a blow to his guts. "The rent's not due for weeks yet."

"Well, it'll be paid early, so it will."

As one, the men of the village surged forward to challenge O'Callaghan. One of the men with him lifted a pistol: "No further, or I fire!"

They all fell back, except for Michael. Every one of them knew that the man meant what he said. Joe Ryan tugged Michael back. O'Callaghan mounted his horse, turned and rode out of the village at a fast trot.

"Come on," Michael said, "we can block the road at the bend, cut them off."

"They have guns," Old Joe Ryan said.

Michael was so angry that he was not afraid of their bullets. He turned and began to run across the fields to the place more than a mile away where the road turned back on itself. After a moment, he realized that he was not alone.

"I'm with you," Liam panted.

"So am I," Sean Ryan said.

About fifteen of the village men were following him. When they reached the road, Michael began to dismantle the stone dyke and lay the stones across the road. The others helped; soon, they had a barricade.

"What do we do now?" Sean Ryan asked.

"Wait," Michael said.

In the distance, they could hear the sound of O'Callaghan's horses. Shortly afterwards, he rounded the bend in the road and saw them.

O'Callaghan stopped. "What's this, then?"

Michael faced him squarely, his arms folded. "All we want is our money, O'Callaghan, or our oats back."

"I made you a fair deal, O'Shea."

"You did not. We sold the oats for cash, not a credit against the rents."

"Same thing."

"It is not. We'd not have sold to you, if we'd known the money was going straight to Fraser. What are you paying him? Fifteen shillings to the pound, something like that?"

"It's not your business, O'Shea. Now, get these rocks out of my way!"

"No." Michael stood firm, refusing to budge.

"I'm warning you, O'Shea…"

"There's more of us than there is of you, O'Callaghan. Just give us the money or let us have the oats back and that'll be the end of it."

O'Callaghan turned to his men. "Seems to me this is highway robbery."

"That's right," the man said. He spoke with a thick, northern accent. He took his pistol out of its holster, aimed at Michael. Michael did not flinch.

"I'm warning you for the last time, O'Shea…"

"We struck a bargain, O'Callaghan. All we want is for you to stick to your side of it."

O'Callaghan's henchman fired, a glancing blow that just nicked the side of Michael's arm, but the force of it drove him back. He felt the sting of the bullet's cut. Behind him, he sensed that the village men were wavering. The pain of the wound in his arm was acute.

"Next time, I shoot to kill."

"What kind of a man are you, O'Callaghan?" Michael asked angrily. Liam tugged at his shoulder, told him to forget it. Blood was streaming down his arm.

"Now, get these stones out of the way," O'Callaghan said.

"To hell with you." Both Liam and Sean were trying to pull him back. Michael turned, his shoulders slumped despondently. "To hell with you, O'Callaghan!" he roared. He strode away, leaving O'Callaghan to remove the stones himself.

Back at the cottage, his mother cleaned the cut in his arm, then she made a poultice of herbs, which she bound to it with a strip of cotton.

"I'm that glad you're back," she said, "I was that feart he would kill you."

Michael said nothing. He saw the tracks of tears on her cheeks, knew that she had been crying. For a moment, he wished that he was a boy again, so that he could give way to the pain he felt inside and cry too.

"It doesn't matter," his mother said, "we'll manage. We'll get through."

Half of the village had been relying on the money from the oats to pay fares to England to find work; the other half needed the money to buy Indian meal, which was much cheaper than oats.

"Ach," Michael said, "I'll go anyway. I'll find work somewhere, get the money somehow."

"You will not," his mother said. "The streets of Dublin are full of beggars. There's no work to be had, for love or money. You're not leaving here without your fare."

She gave him some of the tea that she made from wild herbs that she gathered. The brew was bitter; he drank slowly. He had never drunk real tea; they could not afford it. Vaguely, he wondered what it tasted like.

"I should've known," he said. "I should've known

O'Callaghan had a trick up his sleeve."

"How could you have known, Michael? Besides, it was my fault. It was me who told you to sell to him."

He shrugged. It did not matter now. Nothing mattered now. The hope he had felt a few days ago had proved to be forlorn.

Chapter 10

Elizabeth found him a couple of days later. He was at the riverbank, but he was not trying to guddle trout, he was sitting on the bank, staring up at the moon. Even from a distance, Elizabeth could sense his hurt. She held back, wondering if she should disturb him, if he wanted her to.

With her brothers at home, it was not so easy to slip out of the castle. William and Albert made a habit of staying up late, drinking and playing cards. William had caught her trying to slip out of the castle; Elizabeth had made the excuse that she was hungry, that she was going to the kitchen to get some cocoa and biscuits. William looked at her as if she was going mad; he asked her why she had not just rung for the maid. Elizabeth said that she did not like to disturb her so late.

After that, she had to be very careful. She asked Jamie to deliver the meal by himself; she had only managed to sneak out that night because her brothers went to bed early as they were going shooting in the morning.

Michael sensed her presence. He turned round, smiled wanly, and patted the grass beside him. She went over and sat down.

"How are you, *mavourneen?*"

She smiled, as she always did when he used that word.

"I'm fine, Michael. And you?"

"Ach." Tersely, he told her about the oats, and what had happened with O'Callaghan.

Elizabeth frowned. "You should've told me, Michael. There's plenty of carts in the stables. Jamie could've lent you one, and a horse."

Michael cursed. He had not thought of asking her. "It doesn't matter now," he said after a while. "The oats are gone, and I won't be going to Liverpool. I don't have the fare."

"How much is the fare?"

"Don't ask, Elizabeth. I won't take money from you."

"It could be a loan, Michael. You could pay me back."

He looked at her, smiled sadly. "You know..." he said, then his voice tailed off.

"What do I know?"

"Nothing," he said. He had been going to say that, if things were different, he would be courting her, but he realized how foolish he would sound. He did not have the wherewithal to court anyone, certainly not the daughter of the castle.

"If I could get the money, would you borrow it?" she asked him.

"I don't know. I suppose," he said. Thinking of his family, of how great their need was, he could not refuse. "I'd pay you back," he said quickly. "I'd only need five shillings or so and they say railway labourers get ten shillings a week."

Elizabeth was sure that she could get the money somehow, even if she had to ask her father for a shilling at a time.

"Is there anything else you need, Michael?"

"No, Elizabeth. Just keep on coming to see me, if you can. I like talking to you."

"I like talking to you, Michael."

Elizabeth rode back to the castle slowly. She wondered what had happened to the money from the locket she had given the priest; he had been sure that would be enough to pay the rents. Fraser hated the tenants, though; she knew that. He would do anything he could to trick them out of money.

In the morning, at breakfast, her father's expression was jovial. "The accursed rebels are all in jail," he said. "I've just had word from the garrison commander. It all ended up in a rout in some poor woman's cabbage patch. The rascals fled, apparently. I always knew they were a bunch of cowards."

Lady Roscawl said nothing.

"So it's quite safe for you to travel, my dear, if you still want to go to London."

Elizabeth's mother looked at her father icily. "As you know, I wrote to the Cavendishes to invite them to the shoot. They've accepted our invitation, subject to being able to travel safely, and now I'm sure they can. Of course, I shall have to stay to prepare for them."

There was always a shooting party at Roscawl in August. The men went out after pheasants; their wives stayed in the castle mostly, gossiping and drinking tea. When Elizabeth was a child, she had loved the shoots because her brothers were beaters and sometimes she went with them; she loved roaming the moors, although she felt sorry for the birds who got shot. Now, though, she had to stay in the castle with the women and she found that boring. Her heart sank at the prospect of being in the company of Edward Cavendish, even if only at dinner.

"By the way, Elizabeth," her mother said. "Since we're not going to London yet, I've asked the seamstress to come and make you some new dresses. She'll be here this afternoon."

Elizabeth nodded obediently.

After breakfast, she put on her riding clothes, then took her horse and rode out of the castle grounds. She was heading for the priest's house in the village beyond Roscawl, but she found him walking along the track from the castle, his shoulders slumped despondently.

Elizabeth dismounted and walked to his side.

"Hello, Father."

"What can I do for you, Miss Elizabeth?" he asked, tiredly.

She wished that he would not call her "Miss"; she asked him not to. He smiled wanly.

"It's the rents, Father," she said. "I thought you said that the money from the locket would be enough, but they've taken the money from the oats as well."

"It's that accursed Fraser," he said. "I paid him the money, fifteen pounds I got. I sent the locket to the bishop and he got a good price for it. It paid the rent for the village and a bit against the arrears, but it wasn't enough for him. Aye, but he's a bad 'un. Forgive me, Miss Elizabeth, but I haven't got a good word to say about the man."

"My father said that if anything was paid, just a little, that was enough."

"It might be enough for him, but it wasn't enough for Fraser. Only the Lord knows what we're going to do now. The winter's coming, there's no food stored and the meal from the Poor Law isn't enough. You see, people were hoping that with the money from the oats, some of the lads could get away to England. If they could earn a wage, then they could buy food, pay the rents as well."

"You could talk to my father."

"That's just it, Miss Elizabeth. I went to the castle and asked to see him, but they said I couldn't. If it was to do with the estate, I'd to see Fraser. He's in charge."

"Who did you see?"

"Some lad, a young man with an English accent."

Elizabeth thought. The priest was probably talking about Brown, her father's clerk.

"Fraser tricked you," she said.

"Aye, but what do to about it? Lord Roscawl won't talk to me. Can you talk to him?"

Elizabeth hesitated. She was still not supposed to go out beyond the home farm boundaries; her father would be furious if he knew that she had been speaking to the tenants, or even the priest. "It would be difficult," she said. "I'd have to be very careful."

The priest looked at her sadly. "I thought so," he said.

"I can always try," she said quickly.

"If I could just speak to him," he said. "I mean, surely to goodness, he wouldn't see the people starving. If they just had a chance to earn some money, then the rents, arrears and all, would be paid."

Elizabeth rode back to the castle slowly. She thought for a

while, decided that she could tell her father that she had bumped into the priest when he was on his way back from the castle. Brown was very officious, highly protective of the lord's time. Probably her father did not even know that the priest had called to see him.

Boldly, she knocked at his study door, waited for him to tell her to come in. Lord Roscawl smiled when he saw her, as he always did. "Hello, my dear. What can I do for you?"

"I was out for a ride, Father," she blurted, "when I met the priest. He said that he'd come to see you, but you wouldn't see him."

"Of course not," Lord Roscawl said. "It was an estate matter, apparently, something to do with the tenants. He well knows that he has to see Fraser about things like that."

"But he wanted to see you."

"Elizabeth, he has no business seeing me. Estate matters are dealt with by Fraser. And he most certainly has no business pestering you."

"He didn't pester me. I saw him. I asked him what he was doing."

"Well, whatever it was, it was nothing to do with you."

Elizabeth looked at her father, decided that he was irritated, but not angry. "But you see, Father, Fraser took the money from the oats to pay the rents."

"Well, of course he did. This isn't a charity we're running here."

"But if the tenants had some money they could go to Liverpool and find work. Then they'd be able to feed themselves and pay the rents."

Lord Roscawl sat back in his chair. "Elizabeth, really, this has nothing to do with you."

"But if you could let them have the money, their fares to Liverpool, they'd pay you back. Really they would."

He frowned. "Elizabeth! Truly, this is none of your business. For your information, the Irish peasant is a scallywag. Give him the fare to Liverpool, and you'd never see him again. The rascal would probably drink it all away at an inn in Dublin before he even crossed the Irish sea. I'm most annoyed with the Father for pestering you. I've been very good to the Popish Church. You know we gave them their land for the church. We've never charged a penny rent. As for the tenants, they only just managed to pay their rents. The arrears still stand. I've been highly indulgent with them. Anyone else would have turfed them out long ago."

"But Father…"

"I won't hear another word, Elizabeth. It's none of your concern, none of your concern at all. I know you have a kind heart, but in this case your sympathies are misguided. Tenants are tenants. It's only right and fair that they should pay rent."

Why should they? Elizabeth thought. You don't pay rent; it's only chance that you own the land and not them. It's neither right nor fair that people have to pay rent when they are facing starvation.

She knew that she could not argue further, so she just smiled and got up and left.

One thing that her father said stuck in her mind. The rents were only just paid, he'd said; the arrears were still outstanding. Yet the money the priest had given Fraser should have paid off quite a bit of the arrears, since the rents had been paid with the money from the oats.

It did not make sense. Elizabeth knew that the rent payments were noted in a ledger that was usually in her father's study. She decided to have a look at it when she had a chance.

The dressmaker came and showed her swatches of cloth for her new dresses. Elizabeth hardly cared; her mother came in and chose one in a velvet, another in a burgundy satin.

"It's not a new wardrobe we want," she said haughtily to the dressmaker, "just enough to get her through until we go to London."

At dinner, her mother and father talked about the coming shoot. There were to be more than a dozen guests; that was no problem, since there were many guest rooms in the castle. Lady Roscawl had sent for an ensemble to come from Dublin, to play music. Shoots were suddenly fashionable, since Queen Victoria had expressed a fondness for country pursuits.

Extra girls would be taken on from the village to help care for the guests; some of the boys would get a couple of days' work as beaters. Elizabeth was pleased about that, although she knew they would only get paid a pittance.

After dinner, Elizabeth and her mother had coffee in the drawing-room. As always, Lady Roscawl made polite conversation. Fleetingly, Elizabeth wondered if her mother truly cared about anything, if she had any real feelings at all.

"Tell me," Lady Roscawl said, "what did you make of the heroine of *Vanity Fair*?"

"I, er…" Elizabeth began. Although her mother had given her the book weeks ago, she had not read it. The first few pages had bored her; she had no interest at all in the antics of Becky Sharp.

"I couldn't help have a grudging regard for her," Lady Roscawl said. "She was so utterly determined. She let nothing stand in her way. She decided to better herself, and that is what she did. Don't you think, Elizabeth?"

"I, er, she was rather scheming, wasn't she?"

"Well, yes, but we women have to be scheming, if we want to get our way. I take it the book did not appeal to you?"

"No."

"You have to read it before the shoot, Elizabeth. Everybody is talking about it. You know, sometimes I despair of you."

"Why?"

"You seem to have no interest in society, in fashion. Sarah couldn't wait to go to London, to all the balls. You don't seem to care."

"I like Ireland, Mother. I like living here."

Lady Roscawl looked at her stonily. "I see you still have some growing up to do."

Elizabeth excused herself as soon as she decently could. Hearing her father's voice coming from the smoking-room, she went along to his study. There, she searched for the ledger in which details of the rents were kept, but she could not find it. She went to bed, feeling frustrated.

In the morning, she found Albert in the library reading a copy of *The Times*. When he saw her, he put the paper down.

"Dashed pointless even reading it," he said, "by the time it gets here, it's nearly a week old."

"Albert," she asked him, "where's the rent book for Roscawl kept?"

"Why ever do you want to know?" he asked her.

"Eithne's saved up some money from her wages. She wants to pay something off her cousin's arrears," Elizabeth lied; she had known he would ask, that was the best excuse she could think up.

"The rent book's kept in the factor's office – what's his name? Fraser? All Eithne has to do is talk to him."

Elizabeth thanked him and left. The office was in the house where Fraser lived, just beyond the boundaries of the home farm. Elizabeth walked there after lunch – she had to wait until late in the afternoon before she saw Fraser leaving on horseback.

She walked boldly up to the front door, knocked, then opened it and walked in as if she owned the placed which, in a sense, she did.

Fraser's maid, a thin, harried-looking girl, met her in the hallway. "Why, Miss Elizabeth, what are you doing here?"

"I've come for the rent book," she said brightly. "My brother wants to have a look at it."

"It's in the office and the office's locked," the maid said.

"You have a key, don't you?"

The maid hesitated. "I don't know, I'm not supposed to go in the office when Mr Fraser isn't here."

"My brother will be very annoyed if he doesn't see the book," Elizabeth said firmly.

"Very well then, Miss Elizabeth."

The maid got a key and opened the door of the office, which was just off the hall. Elizabeth went in and looked around.

"The book's in the desk drawer," the maid said.

Elizabeth opened the drawer, found a leather-bound ledger. "I won't be long," she said.

Outside the house, she sat down behind a stone dyke and opened the book. It started in 1836 and noted the rents for tenants in Roscawl and the other two villages on the estate. Elizabeth turned to 1848, ran her finger down the list of tenants for Roscawl. Each was noted as having paid that year's rent, but nothing had been deducted from the arrears. It was as she had suspected; Fraser had not paid the money from the priest to the rents, he had simply stolen it.

She took the book back to the maid, thanked her.

"I'll tell Mr Fraser you were here," the maid said.

"Don't bother. I'm sure William will have a word with him."

She walked back to the castle slowly, wondering what she could do.

Chapter 11

Elizabeth felt so utterly alone. In the castle, there was nobody to talk to, nobody who could give her advice. She wanted to tell her father about Fraser's theft, but he would want to know how she knew what she did, and when she told him that she had given her locket away he would be furious. It would be the word of the priest against that of Fraser; of the two of them, she thought that her father would believe Fraser. The factor would not just confess to his theft.

In the morning, she sat in the library, watching Albert read the paper. The room was in the new wing of the castle and had big picture windows which let in a lot of light and a wonderful view of the hills beyond the home farm.

Albert was engrossed for a while, then he looked up at her: "You're not reading, Elizabeth. Why?"

"I'm thinking," she said slowly.

"What about?" he smiled.

"They were going to evict Roscawl," she blurted out. "'Cept Father said if the tenants paid something, anything towards the rent, he'd let them stay…"

"I don't see what that's got to do with you," he said.

"Well, I didn't want them to get evicted, so I gave my gold locket to the priest and he sold it and gave Fraser the money. But Fraser didn't credit it to the rents, he's still threatening to evict the tenants. Don't you see, Albert? Fraser just stole the money."

Albert said nothing for a moment. He stood up and began to pace the room.

"Albert, will you tell Father? Will you tell him that Fraser's a thief?"

He stopped pacing and stared at her. "Elizabeth, what is it with you and the tenants?"

She blushed and looked away from him. "Nothing, Albert."

He reached out and turned her head back so that she faced him. "There's something, Lizibeth. There's something going on. You aren't … it's not a boy, is it?"

She bit her lip. "He's just a friend."

"Elizabeth! For pity's sake, have you any idea what Pater would do if he knew? He'd have a fit…"

"Albert, *Albert*!" She stopped abruptly, aware that she was shouting. "He's just a friend," she said, in a quiet voice. "I've known him for years."

"Lizibeth, for your own good, you have to stop seeing him. You have to stop now. You have to, else…"

His voice tailed off. She stared at him. "Else what, Albert?"

"I'll tell Pater."

"You wouldn't."

He put his hands in his pockets. "I would. I *should* tell him, anyway."

Thoughts whirred around her mind. She took a deep breath. "If you do, Albert, I'll tell him that you've known for ages."

"You wouldn't."

"I would. Who knows which one of us he'd believe? Do you really want to risk it?"

They faced each other angrily for a while, until Albert shook his head. "Have it your own way, Lizibeth, but, for your own good, I think you should stop seeing him." He turned away and went back to his chair, where he sat down and picked up the paper.

"You won't tell Father, then?"

"No, but I don't think you should go on seeing him."

"What about my locket? What about Fraser?"

"I don't know, Elizabeth. You won't take my advice, so what's the point of me saying anything? Apart from, of course, to warn you that no good will come of this."

Elizabeth slipped out of the library, hurt by his coldness, but relieved that he would not tell her father.

For hours, she roamed the corridors. Roscawl Castle was vast, it had more than a hundred rooms. The maids were hard at work in the guest wing, preparing for the guests who would come to the shoot. Elizabeth went up to the top floor of the old wing and gazed out of a window at the land that stretched out before her. The top floor was not used now, the air was musty and stale. In the old days, she knew that soldiers had slept there, the soldiers who defended the castle against the Irish hordes.

The rooms were poky, lit dimly by small windows. The furniture was old-fashioned, heavy, bare wood. One room was stacked with paintings, landscapes mostly, the oil strokes yellowed by time. Elizabeth looked through them; at the end of the pile she found a portrait. It was of a woman; the hair caught her eye, it was fair, like hers. Their faces were remarkably similar. If the dress had not been so unfashionable, she could have been looking at a picture of herself. On the bottom of the frame, she saw an inscription: Grainne, Lady Roscawl, 1789.

It was a portrait of the Irish Lady. She stared at it for ages. Now she knew Grainne's background, she knew why her picture was not on display with the other ones. Because of Grainne's Irishness, her family were ashamed of her.

Elizabeth was pleased that she looked like her ancestor.

The day passed slowly. Elizabeth spent the time ploughing through a copy of *Vanity Fair*. Her mother would be bound to question her about it; she did not want to give her any reason to be annoyed. When night-time came, she slipped out of her room, then down the stairs. She crept past the smoking-room where her brothers were still playing cards, then went to the stables where Jamie hitched the cart up for her.

She only had a sack of Fraser's meal to give away; Mrs Murphy had said that with the shoot coming up, there was no spare cheese or ham, although there would probably be plenty afterwards.

The journey to the village did not take long; she took the track that went along the riverside, but she did not see Michael. She was disappointed.

After she had given out the meal, she turned and headed for home. His whistle stopped her at the edge of the village; her spirits lifted, she got down from the cart and waited for him.

He was winded when he caught up with her. "Let's sit down for a minute," he said.

They sat on a stone dyke.

"I thought you'd be at the river."

He shook his head. The head gamekeeper had warned him that if he was seen poaching once more, he would be prosecuted. Michael had decided not to risk it, for a week or two at least. If he was in jail for poaching he was no good to his family.

"How are you, *mavourneen*?"

She took a deep breath, told him about Fraser, what had happened with the money from her locket. She did not tell him about Albert.

The expression on his face changed, became hard and angry.

"What can I do, Michael?"

"Nothing. I don't think there's anything you can do. Even if you told your father about the locket, he'd likely still believe Fraser against the priest. The most he'd do is give him the sack, and then there'd just be another bastard to take his place. He'd not give us the rents back, for sure."

They sat in silence for a while.

"What I actually asked was, how are you, Elizabeth? I mean, apart from Fraser and that."

She shrugged. "I don't like the life I'm living, Michael."

"Why not?"

"It's not right, it's not fair us living at the castle with plenty of food, and you in the village, without any."

"That's life," he said, bitterly. "You know, hundreds of years ago, we owned the land. Your father's people, your ancestors, they won it in battle. They were the victors, we were the vanquished. Yet if we do what they did, if we fight to get it back, they call us rebels, put us in jail or shoot us."

"You see? It's not right."

"I know that. But what to do? We've no guns, we're too weak and hungry to fight. The Young Irelanders, they're talk, no more than that. We're too busy trying to get the food we need to survive."

Elizabeth smiled sadly. "My parents, they want to marry me off. They want me to marry this chap called Edward Cavendish."

Michael's stomach lurched. "And how do you feel about that?"

"I won't do it, not in a thousand years. But I don't know what I can do. If I don't marry Cavendish, they'll want me to marry someone else."

"You could run away. We could run away together, go to America."

Elizabeth gazed at him. "Are you serious?"

"No, *mavourneen*," he said, tiredly. "It's just a dream. The fare to America's too expensive. I can't leave my family. But America's a free country, a republic. Every man has the vote. That's where I'd go, if I had the choice."

Elizabeth was thinking, wishing, dreaming that she could somehow find the fare to America, that Michael could be freed of his obligations to his family. She looked at him, though, and saw that his sense of duty was too strong to let him desert the people he loved.

"They can't force me to get married," she said. "I'd rather be an old maid."

He laughed. "That you'll never be, *mavourneen*."

It was time for her to leave. Michael stood up, held out a hand to help her up. He held her hand for a moment longer than was necessary, then kissed her fleetingly on the cheek.

"God bless, *mavourneen*. Sweet dreams."

"And you, Michael," she said, shyly; she was still dizzy with the shock of his caress.

She rode home, the breeze cooling the flush on her cheeks.

He likes me, he really does, she thought, as she went to bed and fell asleep. Albert was wrong, so wrong. No harm would come to her because she was seeing Michael.

Elizabeth woke up the next day, filled with happiness. She drifted through the morning with a smile on her face, thinking about Michael, dreaming about what it would be like if they ran away to America together. They would have to work hard, she thought. She would have to work as well as him, probably, but the thought of work did not trouble her.

She thought of the comforts of the castle, of the warmth, the ease, the food that was served three times a day to her. Michael and the villagers ate only a thin porridge made from meal; she could cope with that, she thought. The rich food at the castle made her feel greedy and guilty.

She did not enjoy wearing lavish clothes, having her hair elaborately styled; she would rather wear a simple peasant's skirt and blouse and let her hair hang free.

She struggled to remind herself that it was a dream; Michael would never leave his family when they were in such great need. If she just ran away to the village her father would find a way of bringing her back.

But if the potatoes began to grow again, if she could defy her parents and refuse to marry Edward Cavendish... With luck, if he could wait, maybe they would find a way.

Just before noon, a commotion in the stable yard disturbed her reverie. She looked out of her bedroom window, saw that Fraser was screaming at Jamie and the coachmen, who were lined up before him. Fraser had a pistol in his hand, which he was waving threateningly at them. Two of the gamekeepers were standing behind him.

She ran downstairs. Her brothers were standing in the corridor, William laughing, a worried frown creasing Albert's brow.

"What's going on?"

William looked at her. "Nothing for you to trouble yourself with."

"What is it, Albert?"

He looked at William, then at her. "They've … Fraser's found out there's meal missing from the store. He thinks the coachmen have been stealing. He's called the constables. He's trying to get them to confess, but they won't."

A wave of dizziness passed over Elizabeth. She leaned against the wall for support. "But what … what's going to happen?"

William smiled. "They'll go to jail, the lot of them. They might even hang for it."

Elizabeth blinked, gasped.

"They won't hang them," Albert said, quickly, "they don't hang thieves. They'll be deported, most likely."

Elizabeth took a deep breath, tried to will strength into her limbs. She walked towards the door that led to the stable yard.

"Where are you going?" Albert asked her.

"Out for a ride," she said. She had on her riding clothes anyway; she usually wore them in the morning.

She would tell Jamie to saddle her horse, get him away from Fraser that way, then they would work out what to do.

In the yard, she faced the factor squarely. "I need Jamie to saddle my horse," she said.

The factor's manner was deferential but firm. "I'm sorry, Miss Elizabeth, but he's under arrest. You'll have to wait."

Out of the corner of her eye, she looked at Jamie. He returned her glance pleadingly. She knew then that he would not tell on her, that, even if he did, he would not be believed unless she confessed as well. The coachmen just looked bewildered. Every one of them had a wife, a family to support on the meagre wage paid by the castle.

Elizabeth spun on her heel, went back indoors. Albert and William were still slouched against the wall, watching the yard.

Albert was looking at her, as if to say, I told you so. She remembered what her father had said, when she'd told him about the factor selling meal in Cork.

"There's no proof that they took anything," she said.

"Proof?" William gazed at her contemptuously. "They're the only ones who can get into the store, apart from Fraser. He's hardly going to steal his own meal."

Elizabeth left them, went into the library where she sat down to think. There was no choice, really – she could not let innocent men be prosecuted for a crime they had not committed. Especially not Jamie, whose only crime had been to help her. Once she had made the decision, she felt a little better.

She took a few deep breaths to summon her courage, then she walked to her father's study and knocked at the door.

"Not now, my dear," he said, when she came in. "I'm busy with estate business."

Fraser was with him; he must have left the men under the guard of the gamekeepers.

"I have to speak to you, Father."

"Elizabeth, I said I'm busy."

"It's very important," she insisted.

He frowned. "Very well. If you'll just give me a moment, Fraser."

The factor nodded and left. Elizabeth sat down.

"Well, what is it?"

"The meal," she said, "I took it. It wasn't the coachmen or Jamie, it was me."

The lord's frown became an expression of disbelief. "What?"

"I took the meal."

"But … why on earth, Elizabeth?"

She hesitated.

Lord Roscawl drummed his fingers on the desk angrily. "I'm waiting…"

"It was, it was a while ago. I'd been out for a ride, and I passed through the village. It was so quiet. I saw this woman, she told me they all had the fever. Most of them were too sick to work on the road. I knew where the meal was stored. That night, I went out to the stables. I took the cart and a couple of sacks of meal and gave it out. I've been doing it ever since."

Her father's face darkened as if a rain storm was passing over him. "How dare you, Elizabeth? How dare you?"

"They were hungry, Father. And sick. They needed food…"

"Have you got any idea of the trouble you've caused? Do you know that the constables are on their way? What am I supposed to tell them – that my own daughter is a thief?"

"Father, I…"

"Get out of my sight, Elizabeth. Go to your room."

"Father…"

"I said, go to your room!"

She went out, closed the door behind her. Fraser had heard the lord's voice raised in anger; he looked at her quizzically. She ignored him.

In her room, she rang for Eithne. When the maid came, there was a worried expression on her face.

"There's terrible trouble, Miss Elizabeth," she said.

"I know. Don't worry about it. Will you go downstairs and try to find out what's happening?"

The maid left. Elizabeth looked out of the window, but she could see nothing. The coachmen were no longer in the yard; she did not know whether that was good or bad. Inside, she was trembling. She looked at herself in the mirror, brushed a stray strand of hair away from her eyes.

Eithne came back a while later. "You've to go down and see the lord, Miss Elizabeth."

"What's happening?"

Eithne shook her head. "I don't know. All I know is I heard Mr Fraser sending a man off to tell the constables they're not wanted after all."

Elizabeth went downstairs to the study. Her father was furious; she had never seen him as angry as that. In fact, when she thought about it, she realized that it was very rarely that he was angry at all. Few people dared to cross Lord Roscawl.

She moved to sit down.

"Stand up," he roared, so loudly that she shook with the shock of his voice. "Don't sit down until I tell you to!"

Elizabeth stood.

"Who helped you, Elizabeth?"

"Nobody, Father. I was on my own."

"Elizabeth, I'm warning you. Somebody must have helped you, and I want to know who."

"Nobody helped me," she insisted.

"You're not strong enough to hitch up the cart by yourself. You don't know how to. And you couldn't carry a sack of meal."

"I can, Father. I am strong enough to hitch up the cart by myself. Of course I know how, I've watched it done hundreds of times."

He was glaring at her.

"If you don't believe me, I'll show you," she said, defiantly. Whatever she did, she had to protect Jamie.

He shook his head slowly from side to side. "You're not even sorry, are you?"

"I … no, I'm not. The villagers needed food, they were starving. I fed them."

"The villagers are not your concern," he said, coldly. "It's certainly not true that they were starving. There's plenty of food for them through the Poor Relief scheme, and if they can't work then they can always go to the workhouse, where they'll be fed. Anything that says that Ireland is starving is just vicious propaganda."

Elizabeth clenched her fists in anger. She had seen the truth with her own eyes. What about the people who were too sick to walk the fifteen miles to the nearest workhouse?

What was supposed to happen to them?

"The Irish peasant is idle by nature," Lord Roscawl went on. "You just encouraged his sloth, Elizabeth."

She thought of Michael and the others working on the road, knew then how wrong her father was.

"If you weren't my daughter, you'd go to jail for this. I've a mind to let you answer for your crimes, even though you are my daughter. But the scandal would hurt your mother greatly. You will go to your room and stay there, Elizabeth. You will have your meals there. You will not come out for any reason unless and until I say so."

"What about the coachmen and Jamie?" she blurted. "What are you going to do with them?"

"That's none of your concern," he said, icily. "If you had any concern for the staff, you should have thought of them before you began your campaign of pilferage."

Elizabeth opened her mouth to plead with him about the villagers, but she knew that anything she said would only make matters worse, so she did not say anything.

"Do you understand?"

"Yes, Father," she said meekly.

She went upstairs, threw herself down on her bed, wondered what on earth she was going to do now.

After a while, there was a knock at the door.

"Come in," she said.

Albert stood there, smiling sadly. "I didn't tell," he said.

"I know you didn't."

"Lizibeth…"

"I know, you told me so."

"I wasn't going to say that."

"What were you going to say?"

"That I'm sorry, that's all. Pater will cool down in a bit, you'll see."

Chapter 12

A bad feeling settled over Michael in the early afternoon; he knew that something was wrong. He was working on the road with the other men from Roscawl, digging the earth and manoeuvring stones out of the way. Although each man had a spade, there was only one pick between them and so he had to work with his bare hands. The work was tiring, his back ached and so did his arms. There were blisters on his hands that could not heal because the work was never-ending; at night they would form scabs which would fall off the next day when he began work again. In the evening, his mother bathed the blisters and bandaged them with healing herbs to prevent them from getting infected. Michael was terrified that his blisters would get infected; if they did he could not work and his family needed the meal to eat.

At the end of the day, he stood in line for the meal that he had earned. Fraser was standing with the overseer from the Poor Law – vaguely Michael wondered why the factor was there. The first man went forward, was given some meal.

"Wait a minute," he said, "I've children to feed. I get more than that."

"No, you don't," Fraser said. "Nobody does. Stolen meal

was given out in Roscawl. Until the loss is made good everybody's on half-rations."

A murmur spread through the waiting men.

Fraser folded his arms and glared at them. "Receiving stolen property is an offence. Would you rather I called the constables in?"

"Our children need to eat," old Joe Ryan said.

"Let them eat the stolen meal then," Fraser told him.

The men walked back to the village, shoulders slumped, despairing. Old Joe and one of the other men went to see the priest, to ask him if there was anything to do. "It's not fair," Joe said, "we didn't know the meal was stolen."

Michael thought that most people had a little meal saved, maybe they could manage through, if they ate a little less. The trouble was that most people were eating just enough to survive; they were stick thin, all of them.

He hated eating the porridge made from the meal anyway; he hated having to live on the grudging charity of the landlords. That night, he ate only a little, gave the rest to his brothers.

Every day, all day, his mother and the other women of the village scoured the land for food. They gathered wild carrots, mushrooms, brambles, only a little, not enough to keep anyone alive. In the old days, before the hunger, occasionally his father had enough money to buy a little sugar and his mother would make bramble jam; now, of course, there was no sugar and the brambles tasted bitter.

Michael walked out into the evening; the cottage was full of his brothers and sisters and he wanted some peace so that he could think. If the missing meal had been discovered, then something had happened to Elizabeth. He wondered what, if she could still come to see him and, if not, how he could get a message to her.

Way along the track, he came across Jamie. The stable-lad was walking along, shoulders hunched, hands in pockets.

"What happened?" Michael asked him.

Jamie shrugged. "Got the sack, didn't I?"

Jamie was an orphan, Michael knew. He had worked at the castle for years, since he was a boy. The stables was just about the only home that he had known. Usually, Michael was distrustful of people who worked at the castle, but he liked Jamie.

"Fraser discovered there was meal missing from the store," Jamie said. "He called the constables, he was going to have us all arrested. Then something happened, like. I don't know what, but I think Miss Elizabeth must have told them it was her who took the meal. So he sent word to the constables not to come. But I got the sack anyway. He said I was neglecting my duty, letting someone into the stables to take a horse and cart when I was asleep. He never knew I helped her. He said if he thought I had, then he'd have me jailed for it. I was lucky he was just giving me the sack, he said…" Jamie shrugged, tried to smile though Michael could see the hurt on his face.

"What happened to Elizabeth?"

Jamie shook his head. "I don't know. I've no idea. All hell broke loose, see? When Fraser was in with the Lord, he left us with the gamekeepers and one of the coachmen, he decides to run. I mean, the gamekeepers wouldn't shoot him. So he runs away and the young master gets to hear about it. Next thing, he wants to organize a man hunt.

After an innocent man, you know? Whooping and laughing, he was."

Michael felt sick at the thought of it. He was also terribly worried about Elizabeth. Jamie knew nothing, though, he realized.

"What are you going to do?" he asked him.

"Just walk. I thought I'd head for Cork, get a ship to America."

"You have money?"

"Only sixpence. I'll have to stow away, or work my passage. But I might find work on the way. I'm a good stable-lad." He grinned cheerfully.

It was more than fifty miles to Cork, a good day's walk. Jamie only had the clothes he stood up in and a decent pair of boots, thank goodness.

"I could let you have a little food," Michael said. There was smoked trout at home; his manners demanded that he could not let Jamie go all that way without something to eat.

"Don't be daft," Jamie said. "I was well fed at the castle. Full up, so I am. It won't hurt me not to eat for a day or two."

With a jaunty wave, he walked off towards the sunset. He would be all right, Michael knew; Jamie had the mark of a survivor. For a moment, he envied him for his freedom, for his lack of responsibilities, then he set off for the river, to poach some trout. His family still had to be fed, and with the reduced rations of meal from the road, they would have to eat some of the smoked and salted fish they had stored for the winter.

*   *   *

120

When the word spread that Jamie had been sacked and one of the coachmen had left, the villagers realized that there would be work at the castle. The next day, Liam and Niall queued up at the gates to the stable yard, with some of the other men and most of the boys. Michael did not go because he had been with his father that day that the factor had accused him of giving up cheek and he knew that he would be judged guilty by association. In days past, when the potatoes were growing, the village men had considered work at the castle to be the last resort; they valued their independence greatly, but times had changed and any one of them would have given his right arm for the chance of a job.

Fraser scanned the line arrogantly. "Any of you got experience as a coachman?" he asked them.

Nobody had.

"I'm not going to hire an unskilled man," he said. Disconsolately, the men turned away and headed for the roadworks.

Fraser turned to the boys. "Any of you got experience with horses?"

Liam and Niall both put their hands up; their father had once owned a horse and they could ride and hitch up a cart.

"You," Fraser pointed at Liam. "Can you saddle a horse?"

"No, but I know how to handle one. I could learn, easily." Liam's spirits rose. If he got the job at the castle, he could really help Michael care for his family; he knew that the burden was heavy on his brother.

Fraser looked him up and down. "Name?"

"Liam O'Shea."

"Brother of Michael?"

Liam nodded.

"Away out of here," Fraser said curtly. "The O'Sheas have the name of being troublemakers."

Liam told Michael all about it at dinner, after the day's work on the roads was done. Michael's face hardened; he realized that O'Callaghan must have told the factor about his attempts to get the oats back, or at least cash money for them. The scar on his arm twinged.

"It doesn't matter," he said. "It only pays a pittance. You'd not get much more than your room and board."

Liam told him that he had heard at the castle that the coachman had come back, but Fraser would not let him keep his job. The factor said that if the coachman had run away, there must be something that he felt guilty about.

Michael swore; his mother rebuked him softly.

That night, he could not sleep for thinking about Elizabeth, worrying about what was happening to her.

The priest came to the village the next day, after the work on the road was over. The villagers gathered around him; he said that he had been to Fraser to protest about the reduced meal but that the factor had been adamant that the rations would be cut until the loss was made up. Father O'Shaughnessy said that he had written to the bishop about it, to ask him to take it up with the Poor Law Board, but he doubted if the bishop's intervention would make any difference. Fraser was too powerful; on the vast estates owned by Lord Roscawl, the factor's word was law.

The priest said a prayer, the villagers bowed their heads and prayed with him.

After the prayer was over, Michael went up to the priest. "Father, I…"

"What is it, Michael?"

"I'm worried about Elizabeth," he blurted.

Father O'Shaughnessy smiled. "I was thinking of her too. I've prayed for her, of course. She'll be all right, I should think. I doubt they'll punish her. What could they do?"

Michael hoped and prayed that Elizabeth would have the courage to stand up to her parents.

On the way back to the cottage, he overheard some of the other villagers criticizing Elizabeth, saying that she should not have interfered, that they would be better off if she hadn't. Angrily, he strode up to them. "How dare you speak ill of her? She's the only one who cares for us."

"Aye, but look where her efforts have got us."

Michael shook his head, walked away.

In the cottage, their neighbour, Maeve O'Rourke, was talking to his mother. Maeve was a widow too, but her husband had died before the hunger. She had a family of six – only one son, the rest were daughters. Although her son worked on the road and he was supposed to get enough meal to feed them all, the O'Rourkes often went hungry. Their cow had died in the spring; they no longer had milk. Michael's mother always shared what she could with them, but there was not enough to go around.

The women looked up as Michael walked in. He sensed he had interrupted something, turned to walk out again.

"No, Michael, don't go," Maeve said.

He sat down on a stool by the fire. The only thing that they had enough of was peat to heat the cottage. In July,

Michael and his brothers had cut peats from the bog, they were drying in stacks outside the cottage now.

"Maeve's going to leave," his mother said. "She's going to head for the workhouse at Cork."

He looked at her. Maeve's thin face was threaded with worry lines, she was wringing her hands in anguish.

"It's the best thing to do," she said, trying to smile. "The weather's good and there's space for us, Father O'Shaughnessy said. It's the best thing to do."

He saw the sadness behind her smile, knew that she did not want to go.

"You don't have to go, Maeve," he said. "You know we'll help. There's always fish in the river, rabbits to trap. You might be hungry, but you'd not starve."

She shook her head slowly. "It's good of you, Michael, but we best go now, when the weather's good. We can walk there in a day or two without any bother. The girls are nearly grown now. In the city, there's a chance they'd get work."

Michael thought of the cottage they lived in, their heritage from the forefathers. It was built of stone, with a heather thatched roof – it was not much but it was a home. Maeve had furniture too – stools, a table, a chest of drawers – unless she had sold it to the tinkers.

"It's Patrick, you see," Maeve said. Patrick was her son. He was just fourteen, but on the roads he was expected to work as hard as men twice his age. One day, something had happened to his back when he tried to move a heavy wheelbarrow; he said that it felt like something had snapped. Michael had seen the pain on his face; ever since then the men had been covering for him, letting him have the easier jobs, but his injury had not healed.

"I don't want him working on the roads with his back."

"I understand," Michael said. "What about your things?"

"We'll take as much as we can. Your mother'll sell the rest, next time the tinkers come."

"I was telling Maeve," his mother said, "that you'll help her along the road if she leaves on Sunday."

"Yes," Michael said. "Of course I will."

"I went to see the factor," she said. "I thought I might get some rent back." She shrugged. "No luck."

Michael thought how unfair it was that the cottage, built by the O'Rourkes, was now considered the property of Lord Roscawl. Fraser would charge the next tenants a price for the cottage, but Maeve would never see a penny of it.

On Sunday, at early Mass, Michael scanned the church for Eithne. He relaxed when he saw her sitting in the front row, with the other maids from the castle.

He was waiting for her when she came out. "Please, can you tell me how Elizabeth is?" he asked her.

Eithne looked around, waited until the other maids had walked a way ahead of them. "She's in a lot of trouble," she said.

"I know that, but is she all right?"

"She's managing," Eithne said.

"Can you get a message to her?"

"What do you want to say?"

Michael thought for a moment. He wanted to tell Elizabeth that he was thinking of her, that he cared for her, but he did not want to tell the maid that. "Just that I asked for her, that I'm thinking of her, that I hope I can see her sometime."

"I'll tell her," Eithne said, "but I doubt you'll be able to see her. She's not allowed out of the castle, you see. She's not even allowed out of her room."

Michael felt sick just thinking about it.

The whole village came out to see the O'Rourkes off. Michael had talked to his mother late into the night about it, realized finally that it was the only thing that they could do, the only chance they had. If they stayed in Roscawl, if Patrick could not work on the roads, then they were facing starvation. Although people would gather round and help them, there just wasn't enough food to go round.

Maeve put a brave face on it. She said the workhouse was the only chance that they had, that the girls were fit and strong, they were bound to find work. If the potatoes started to grow again, they could always come back. The chances were that Fraser would not find another tenant for their tiny patch of land.

As they began to walk towards Cork, Michael saw that Maeve was crying.

"Come on," he said, trying to comfort her, "better times are bound to come."

"I hope so," she sobbed. "Things just can't get any worse."

Chapter 13

Roscawl changed after the O'Rourkes left. The anger that people had felt against the wiles of O'Callaghan and Fraser became a sense of hopelessness; they felt that they no longer had any control over their future. The Young Irelanders' talk of rebellion had come to nothing; Michael had always known that they would fail, but their rout in the cabbage patch became yet another omen of doom.

Only Michael refused to give way to despair; his anger hardened, became a throbbing rage that was with him always, as he worked on the roads. He tried to work it out on the earth and the stones.

Elizabeth was in his mind all the time; he vowed that, somehow, he would see her again. He did not know when or how, only that he had to.

One night, when he got home from the road, his mother was smiling. With the other women, she had walked over the fields of wheat that had just been harvested, gathered all the grain that had been missed. The grain had been ground into flour, there was just enough to make one small loaf.

Michael had not eaten bread for ages; just the thought of it made his mouth water.

"Wait," he said, "I won't be long."

Taking a length of rope with him, he walked out over the hills to one of the farms on the estate. From a distance, working on the roads, he had seen a big herd of cows with their calves. The farmer would not miss one, he thought.

He chose a fine young calf; he made a halter and led it back over the hills to Roscawl. If anyone challenged him, he was going to say that he had found the calf wandering, but nobody did.

The calf followed him trustingly; by the time he got back to the village he was feeling guilty that he had to kill it. He whistled softly to call the other men. One by one, they came out of their cottages.

"Lord's sake, Michael," one said, "you'll have us all in jail."

"It won't be missed," he said. "We'll bury the bones and the pelt."

Swiftly, the calf was killed and butchered, the meat and offal shared out. Nobody had any salt to preserve the meat, so that night the village dined richly on roast beef and freshly baked bread.

Beef was a rare treat in Irish villages; in all of his life, Michael had not eaten it before.

In the morning, he felt that the air of despondency had lifted a little. Well fed, the people did not feel quite so bad.

Carefully, he buried the hide and the bones, so that even if the farmer realized that one of his calves had been stolen, there would be no proof of it. He could not do it again, though; he knew that if he did he would be discovered and that the entire village, all the villages on the estate, would take the blame.

*   *   *

The gamekeepers were patrolling the river. Michael had to walk for miles before he found a place that was clear of them. There, though he waited for ages, no fish swam into his arms. He decided to give up for the night, the moon was high and the sky was clear; perhaps his reflection in the water was scaring the fish away.

The spot he had chosen was close to the castle; when he looked up, he could see its walls rising against the night. He felt the closeness of Elizabeth. On impulse, he walked towards it.

When he passed through the stable yard, a dog barked. He whistled softly, to quieten it. Close to the castle now, he looked up at her bedroom window. He knew which one it was, because he had been there with her, years ago.

He smiled at the memory of his childish prank, ringing all the bells to call the servants. He had been so happy then. Before the potatoes went bad, before the hunger, he had really believed that his dreams could come true.

He picked up a pebble, tossed it at the window. It struck the glass with a sharp ping, but he could see that the heavy curtains were closed, he knew that they would muffle the sound.

For a while, he sat down, trying to will Elizabeth awake, to will her to come to the window. If he could just see her, he would feel better. He was so worried about her, he wanted so much to be able to talk to her, to hear her voice again, to know that she was all right.

In time, he thought, her parents would forgive her. After all, what was a little meal to a man of Lord Roscawl's wealth? It was not as if he had actually lost anything, the meal was being made up by the reduced rations. In time, Elizabeth would be free again, would be able to come to see him.

In the morning, one of the gamekeepers came to the men working on the road. There was going to be a shoot, he said; the estate needed at least a dozen boys to be beaters. They would get paid for it, there would be a couple of days' work at least.

On the way home, the men talked about it. In years past, Michael had been a beater; he had been paid a shiny new penny for his work. He remembered the thrill of earning the money, how proudly he had given it to his father. His father had given it back to him, told him to save it for the future. It was long gone, of course.

"I've an idea," Michael said. "There's no work here, beyond the road, no chance of work either. Why don't we use the money the boys get to send someone to Liverpool? Soon's he gets work, he sends the fare for someone else, and so on. That way, we've a chance, a chance of getting through."

The men looked at each other, murmured their agreement.

"Who goes?" Old Joe Devlin asked.

"Michael should go, it was his idea," Phelim Flanaghan said.

"No," Michael said quickly. He did not want to leave, not until he had heard from Elizabeth. "We'll draw lots for it, decide that way."

If just one man got to Liverpool and found work, the village had hope for the future again.

*　　*　　*

On Sunday in church, Eithne, the maid, smiled at him. Michael felt his heart lift. Afterwards, he waited for her.

"Elizabeth says to tell you that she's fine," Eithne said. "She's allowed out of her room now, so it's not so bad."

Michael was relieved. "Tell her that we're managing too," he said, "I hope I can see her soon."

Eithne looked at him. He was tall, strongly built although he was thin; his clothes were ragged, like all the villagers, and he was barefoot. She was not sure what the relationship was between him and Elizabeth; she sensed that it went beyond friendship. She saw the happiness on his face, thought that he would be bound to get hurt. After all, it was unthinkable that the daughter of the Lord would have anything to do with a village lad. The Lord would never permit it. She decided to try to let him down gently. "Elizabeth will be married, soon, you know," she said. "There's talk of her marrying the young Cavendish."

Michael's face fell. She had told him that, also that she did not want to. "She doesn't want to," he blurted.

"It's not what she wants so much as what her parents want. I don't think she's got so much choice about it," Eithne said. "I just thought I better tell you."

Michael just said, "Oh," then he turned and walked away. Eithne watched him go, thinking that she had done her best.

That night, Michael stood watching the castle. Elizabeth was just a few yards away, on the other side of the walls. The thought of her marrying had nagged at his mind all day. Surely her parents could not force her into a marriage that she did not want?

Very slowly, he crept around the walls, into the kitchen

garden. Carefully, he turned the handle of the door, pushed it open. Inside the kitchen, he waited for a long time until he was sure that he had not been heard, then he walked on tiptoe along the corridor. Halfway along, voices spilled from a room, light leaked from under a door. He waited again, walked past the room smartly when he heard the sound of laughter.

Upstairs, he hesitated; he was not sure which room was Elizabeth's and he did not want to disturb anyone else. He opened the door of a room that was empty before he tried the next one, which was hers.

Elizabeth was asleep, her hair spread over the pillow. A shaft of moonlight came through the space between the curtains, slicing across the bed in which she slept.

Michael shook her gently to wake her.

Her eyes opened, widened in surprise. "Michael?"

"Ssshhh." He held his finger to his lips.

A flush spread over Elizabeth's face; she was wearing only a nightgown, she was a little embarrassed. She reached for the shawl on her night-table and drew it around her shoulders.

"I had to come to see you," he said. "Your maid, she said you might be getting married."

Elizabeth winced. "I don't want to," she said.

"They can't make you, can they?"

Elizabeth thought; she no longer knew. When after a week her father had called her down to his study to let her know that she was allowed out of her room once again, he had told her that she was not allowed out of the castle, not even for a walk, never mind a ride. "But…" she had protested.

He silenced her with a glance of controlled fury. "I'm warning you, Elizabeth," he said, "don't test me. Don't you dare test me."

She was not sure what he meant by that, but she got a hint from Albert.

"It's Mother," he told her. "She's saying that you're mad. She wanted to get a doctor to come to see to you."

Elizabeth gasped. "I'm not mad, Albert. You know that."

"Yes, but…" He shrugged. "You know what Mother's like."

A shiver passed down her spine then. "Albert, you've got to talk to her, tell her that she's wrong."

He smiled sadly. "She doesn't listen to me, Lizibeth. Just be very careful, don't get in her way. Don't upset her, for heaven's sake. She'll calm down in a while."

She knew then that she could not rely on Albert for help.

Tears came to her eyes. "Oh, Michael," she murmured. "I don't know. I just don't know."

He put his arms around her, rocked her gently to comfort her.

"My mother's saying I'm mad."

"You're not mad, *mavourneen*. You're wonderful. Don't you know that?"

"I missed you, Michael."

"I missed you too. Don't worry, they can't make you marry anyone unless you want to."

She felt his strength; she was thinking that she did not want to marry anyone but him.

Michael was wondering what he could say to her. He

could offer her nothing, not even a roof over her head. He knew that if she ran away from the castle, the Lord would send men out to look for her. She would not be safe in Roscawl.

"If you could wait," he said slowly, "could you manage to wait for a month or two?"

Elizabeth thought. A wedding took a long time to arrange; even if she became betrothed to Edward Cavendish now the marriage would not take place until the spring.

"Yes," she said.

"You see, I think I can get my fare to Liverpool…"

"I'm sorry, Michael, I just can't help you."

"Ssshh, *mavourneen*, I didn't ask you to. I can manage to get the fare myself. And once I get there, once I get work, then I can take care of you. I'll come and fetch you as soon as I can."

"I might be in London."

"That would be even better. It's easier to get from London to Liverpool than it is to get there from here."

"Oh, Michael…"

"Sshh, *mavourneen*, we'll find a way."

What worried Elizabeth was the thought that her father might punish the villagers for something she did, like he had punished them because she had taken the meal. She told Michael that.

"Don't worry," he said, "he won't have a clue. Nobody knows about the two of us apart from your maid, and she's not going to tell anyone, is she?"

"No," she said, slowly.

"I'm not rich, Elizabeth." He smiled. "There won't be much money, but I'll take care of you, I promise you that."

They talked into the small hours, until Elizabeth's brothers had gone to bed and the castle was completely silent. Michael told Elizabeth about his dream of going to America; she smiled, told him that she would love to go there with him. He really believed then that his dream might come true.

When it was time to leave, he looked at the window. "Does that open?"

"Yes." She showed him how.

He looked down. The drop was only twelve feet or so.

"Michael, you can't jump. You haven't got any boots on."

He grinned. The soles of his feet were tough after years of walking barefoot. As lithely as a cat he dropped to the ground, then turned and walked away, waving cheerfully to her.

On his way home, he thought of the promise he had made to her. Now he had told her, he had to make it real. He could not bear to think of her as a prisoner in the castle, forced to marry a man who she did not love. Although she had not said so, he thought that she loved him.

Despite all of his problems, all of his troubles, Michael was filled with a sense of joy.

Chapter 14

Elizabeth woke up the next day feeling happy for the first time in ages. She hated being cooped up in the castle, not being allowed to go out. When she had been confined to her room, she felt so trapped that she wanted to scream. Her brothers ignored her, her parents did not speak to her; although she was not close to her mother her father's silent condemnation hurt her.

Now, thinking of her future with Michael, she knew that she did not have to tolerate it for so much longer.

At breakfast, her parents talked about the shoot; the guests were due to arrive later that day and her mother was complaining about the work she had to do, checking each guest room to make sure that it was ready. She did not trust the maids or Mrs Murphy. As always, she made snide remarks about the heathen Irish; Lord Roscawl just smiled indulgently.

Elizabeth hated hearing talk like that; the Irish were not heathen, they were just poor and it was not their fault that they lived in poverty.

Lady Roscawl said, with a sneer, that some of the girls they had taken on from the village to help did not even know how to make a bed properly; Elizabeth wondered if she realized that the tenants could not afford the fine linen sheets that graced every bed in the castle.

After the meal was over, her father turned to her and asked her to come and see him in his study. Elizabeth smiled, hoping that he would perhaps let her go out riding once again. Although she knew that he had been very angry, she hoped that he would now forgive her.

In his study though, the Lord looked at her coldly.

"I trust you'll be on your best behaviour while we have guests to entertain," he said.

"Why ... yes. Yes, of course."

"I hope so. Your mother is concerned. If you misbehave in company it would adversely affect your prospects of marriage."

Elizabeth grinned inwardly, thinking of Michael. She had no intention of marrying anyone her parents chose for her, although of course she could not tell her father that.

"You do realize that, don't you, Elizabeth?"

"Yes, Father." She did not have long to wait; Michael had said it would only be a month or two.

"Very well, then." He was about to dismiss her.

"I'm not mad," Elizabeth blurted.

He stared at her.

"Albert said ... he said that Mother was saying I was."

Lord Roscawl sighed. "Your mother was merely concerned, Elizabeth, as we all are, at your behaviour. She tells me that you have little interest in clothes or in taking your place in society. You must admit that what you did was odd, to say the very least."

Elizabeth looked away; she did not want to say anything. Having seen the village, how thin the villagers were, anyone would want to help, she thought. That her father knew and did not help shocked her; deep inside, she knew that she was right and he was wrong. She could not understand how anyone could be in his position and do nothing.

"You caused me a great deal of embarrassment," he said.

Still, she said nothing.

"What is worse, you have not apologized."

She raised her eyes until they met his. Lord Roscawl was waiting, she knew, for her to say sorry, but she could not say sorry for doing something that she still thought was right.

The silence hung heavily in the room, like a shroud.

"Very well, then," he said finally, to dismiss her.

"Can I go out for a ride, Father?" As soon as she asked the question, she knew that it was stupid.

"No, you cannot, Elizabeth. You will remain within the castle until you and your mother leave for London. If you're at a loss for something to do, then help your mother to make sure we're ready for our guests."

Elizabeth went to the guest wing. Brigid, her mother's maid, told her that Lady Roscawl had gone to lie down for a bit, because she had a headache. The rooms were perfect, though; each one had been dusted and swept, the furniture polished, the beds were freshly made and fires laid in the grates, ready to be lit. The air smelled crisply of beeswax and linen.

"Is it all right, Miss Elizabeth?" Brigid asked her, wringing her hands nervously.

Elizabeth smiled. "It's fine, as far as I can see."

"We've still drinking water to put in the rooms, but we'll do that later, so it's fresh. A bowl of fruit as well, Her Ladyship said."

"Honestly, Brigid, don't worry, you've done a good job."

Elizabeth left the guest wing, walking along the corridors until she reached the old part of the castle, where she went upstairs to the room where Grainne's portrait was stored. She looked at the picture for ages, wondering what Grainne would have done if she had been alive now. She sensed that Grainne would have done what she did, that she would have shared food with the tenants.

Her father's indifference to their plight shocked her. He talked of the meal handed out for the poor relief work on the roads as a great act of charity, as if by doling out that pittance he was doing more than enough.

Elizabeth remembered what Michael had said, that hundreds of years ago, his people, the Irish, had owned the land. Her ancestors had won it by conquest, by force of arms. The Roscawl estates extended to more than a hundred thousand acres; it was not right, she thought, that one man owned it all. There was plenty of land for everyone; he could give each of the tenants enough land to support a family well and not even notice the loss of it.

Maybe it was the time she had spent as a child with Michael and the village children, maybe it was her inheritance from Grainne, but Elizabeth knew then that Michael was right, that the way her father treated the tenants was wrong. For a long time, she had blamed the way the tenants were treated on Fraser, but she knew now that her father was to blame as well.

The knowledge hurt her. Although there had been little affection in Elizabeth's life, her father had always been kind to her. In a distant way, she had loved him, had always thought of him as a good man, as a fair man. It hurt to know that he was utterly indifferent to the plight of the villagers, the people who had faithfully paid him rent for so many years.

She looked at the picture of Grainne, wishing that she could talk to her, to someone who thought the way she did.

The bell for lunch disturbed her. She brushed the dust from her dress and ran downstairs, anxious not to keep her family waiting.

The guests began to arrive in the afternoon. Her father's cousins, the Armstrongs, came first. Their estate was thirty miles to the south, in Waterford, on the other side of the Comeragh mountains. Elizabeth stood politely to welcome them; the Armstrong boys immediately went off with her brothers, her mother and Mrs Armstrong retired to the drawing-room for tea. At a loose end, Elizabeth went to the library, where she read in the paper that the wheat harvest had been one of the best ever.

The other guests arrived soon, the Clarendons and the Stewarts, the Carews, the Brownes and all the rest of them. The women gathered in the drawing-room, the men in the smoking-room. Amongst the women, the talk was of fashion, of the goings-on at the court of Queen Victoria, of her visit to Ireland that had been postponed again. Elizabeth was bored, but she knew better than to show it; she listened politely with a slight smile fixed to her lips.

As the afternoon passed and the Cavendishes did not arrive, she began to hope, but her hopes were dashed when they arrived just after six, apologizing because one of the wheels of their carriage had been damaged and they'd had to stop to change it.

Edward Cavendish smiled shyly at her; Elizabeth shivered inside because he was even less attractive than she remembered him being. The skin of his face was sallow, dotted with spots, his nose was hooked and his chin was non-existent. She glanced at her mother, saw the sycophantic smile fixed to her face as she welcomed the Duchess.

A fleeting thought struck her that perhaps his looks were deceptive, that he might be a nice person underneath his ugly exterior. She wondered if he knew of the plan to marry her off to him.

Before dinner, she went to change into the burgundy satin gown that the seamstress from Cork had made for her. The skirt was very full, the neck cut modestly.

"The colour suits you," Eithne said.

Elizabeth looked at her reflection disinterestedly.

Because of all the guests, they were dining in the great hall. The vast room was lit softly by candles, the silver and crystal on the table glowed. Elizabeth was seated beside Edward Cavendish.

"I must say," he said, "you've grown up since I last saw you."

Elizabeth smiled obediently, but she could not think of a polite reply.

They were served soup, then the fish course, a fillet of salmon in a butter sauce.

"Are you looking forward to the shoot?" she asked him, unable to think of anything else to say. She was aware that her mother's eyes were upon her, that manners demanded that she make conversation.

"Well, actually," he said, "to be absolutely truthful, not

really. I'm not the world's greatest sportsman. I've never quite understood why it's considered to be fun to tramp over damp moors after a bunch of pheasants. It's so much easier to send the gamekeepers after them."

Elizabeth opened her mouth to ask him why he had come, then thought better of it. "Don't you like the countryside?"

"Well, actually, I prefer town. So much more civilized. I don't mean Dublin, of course. I mean London. There's so much more to do. One's friends are there, of course. I spend a lot of time at my club."

"I'm sorry to drag you away from it," Elizabeth said.

"Oh, certainly not. My mother told me that you had become the most delightful young lady and, I must say, she's quite right."

Elizabeth blinked; so he does know, she thought.

He smiled at her, exposing a row of teeth stained brown by tobacco.

"I must say, I'm delighted to make your acquaintance again."

She smiled. "It's very kind of you to say so."

The fish plates were taken away and replaced with ones for the meat. As the food was served, Elizabeth thought, as she always did, of the people just a short way away living on a few ounces of meal a day.

She toyed with her food; having so much made her feel guilty.

"I say, this beef's excellent," Edward Cavendish said. "Aren't you enjoying it?"

"Yes, of course," Elizabeth replied. She looked around, saw that her parents were engrossed in conversations of their own. "You know," she said, in a quiet voice, "the potato crop's diseased, uneatable. It has been for three years. Some grew last year, but not nearly enough."

"I know," he frowned. "It's dashed hard lines. A very sorry state of affairs indeed. Something should be done about it."

Her heart lifted momentarily. Maybe I'm not alone, she thought. Maybe he cares too.

"I do like potatoes," he said. "I really miss them. I just don't like these dumpling things they tend to serve instead. This blight's such a dashed inconvenience."

Elizabeth's heart sank. She knew then that even if Edward Cavendish was the last man on earth, she would never marry him. She was thankful that she did not have to.

All she had to do was wait, she thought. If she could get through the next month or two, then Michael would come for her and they could run away to Liverpool.

She got through the rest of the meal as best she could. Afterwards, as the ladies retired, Edward Cavendish thanked her for her company.

The guests were tired after the journey. Elizabeth was grateful that they went to bed early, that she did not have to sit up for hours making small talk.

Instead, she lay awake in her bed, thinking of Michael.

In the morning, while the men were out shooting, the women gathered in the drawing-room and gossiped. Elizabeth listened with a smile fixed to her face; she was not sure what they were talking about, there were a lot of knowing looks and raised eyebrows. As the daughter of the house, she was supposed to listen but not participate unless a remark was directed to her. This year was the first time she was considered old enough to take part in these gatherings; previously she had been left to her own devices and she wished she could be on her own now.

The talk bored her. After a long time, her interest quickened when she realized that they were talking about the daughter of a judge in Dublin who had run off with a poet, a Catholic no less, rumoured to support the Young Irelanders. The women were shocked, they simply could not understand how a young girl from a good family could do such a thing. Elizabeth smiled to herself, wondering what their reaction would be if they knew of her plans to run away with Michael.

The day passed slowly. After lunch, the Duchess of Cavendish sat down beside her and they had a long conversation about music. Elizabeth sensed that the Duchess was grilling her and she resented the intrusion.

As Eithne helped her dress for dinner, she asked if Elizabeth was enjoying the company.

Elizabeth confessed that she was bored.

"I thought you'd enjoy meeting new people, Miss Elizabeth."

"They all seem the same to me, Eithne. All they talk about is gossip and fashion. They don't seem to…"

"They don't what, Miss Elizabeth?"

Ever since she had been to the village and seen the predicament of the people Elizabeth had been able to think of little else. "They don't seem to know how hungry people are, Eithne. They don't seem to care."

"I suppose they think it's not their business," the maid said.

"But it is. It's everyone's business."

"That's not the way most people think, Miss." She smiled. "You're a good soul, so you are, Miss Elizabeth. I wish there was more like you."

At dinner, the men reported that the shooting had been excellent. Afterwards, the musicians from Dublin gave a concert in the formal blue drawing-room, a room that was bigger and more lavishly decorated than the other drawing-room. The men listened attentively, but Elizabeth sensed that they wanted to get away to their port and cigars, their talk. Lord Clarendon was the Lord Lieutenant of Ireland, the highest government official in the land; she would have liked to know what was going on in his mind, but such matters were not considered to be a lady's business.

During an interval in the music, Edward Cavendish came over and bowed to her mother.

"I must congratulate you, Lady Roscawl, on a most pleasant entertainment."

"How kind of you to say so, Lord Edward."

"Your home is very beautiful. I wonder if I could ask your lovely daughter to show me around?"

"Of course you can." Lady Roscawl looked at Elizabeth, who knew she would incur her mother's wrath if she refused.

She showed him through the library, the formal rooms in the new wing, then she led him through to the old wing where she intended to show him the family portraits in the great hall.

He did not seem interested, though, as she pointed to the ancient oil of the first Lord Roscawl.

He cleared his throat. "I say, Elizabeth, I really wanted to get the chance to talk to you alone."

She looked at him, one eyebrow raised.

"You see, my mother thinks – and I agree, of course – that I should ask you for your hand in marriage. What do you say?"

The proposal was so abrupt that she was taken aback for a moment.

"You're the right age," he went on, "and so am I. It would be good for both families, don't you think, what? Our fathers are friends, and our mothers get on so well."

She was wondering what on earth had prompted his interest in her. After all, he hardly knew her, so how could he possibly love her? Surely he would not propose just because his mother thought it was a good idea. Or would he? She looked at him, thinking.

"So, what do you say?"

"I…" She felt trapped, as surely as a rabbit in a snare. "I don't know what to say. You've taken me by surprise."

"Surely you agree that it's a good idea."

"I … I'd like some time to think about it, if you don't mind."

His face fell. "I suppose so, if you must. But I'm sure you'll see the sense of it, when you do."

They went back to the drawing-room. Elizabeth avoided her mother's enquiring glances. She could hardly bear even the thought of marriage to Edward Cavendish, a man so weak that he had no mind of his own, that he meekly followed his mother's bidding. She could not even pretend to like him. A wave of anger rippled through her at her mother, who cared so little for her that she wanted to marry her off to a man who was convenient for her own social ambitions.

It did not matter, she thought. He would assume she was thinking for a few weeks; by the time he would expect an answer, she would be away with Michael.

In the morning, before breakfast, Lady Roscawl sent Brigid with a message to Elizabeth that she wanted to see her. Elizabeth dressed hurriedly and went along the corridor to her mother's dressing-room.

"You wanted to see me, Mother?"

"Yes, Elizabeth." Lady Roscawl turned to Brigid, who had been doing her hair, and dismissed her.

"I hear Edward Cavendish proposed to you."

Elizabeth sighed inwardly. "Yes, mother."

"Elizabeth," she fixed her with a steely glare, "you will accept his proposal."

"But, Mother…"

"No buts, Elizabeth. Your father and I are agreed that the right thing for you to do is to marry him. We will not tolerate any arguments. Your behaviour recently has given us great cause for concern. It is time that you were married. You will tell him today that you accept his proposal and we will begin the arrangements at once. That is all."

After breakfast, Elizabeth spoke to Edward Cavendish in the library.

"I've thought about your proposal," she said, hating every word that she said, but she knew that she did not have any choice, "and I've decided to accept."

"Jolly good," he said, smiling broadly, "Mother will be pleased."

Elizabeth walked along the corridor, her shoulders slumped. Outside the smoking-room, she heard the sound of men's voices.

"I've always felt the House does not understand our problems here in Ireland," her father said.

"Exactly," somebody said. Elizabeth stopped to listen, knowing that they were talking about the goings-on at Parliament.

"I mean," her father went on, "take the typical English tenant. He is loyal to the core. If you need to raise an army, he will fight to the death. If the army had to rely on the Irish, God help us. If they fight at all, they fight for the other side."

"That's absolutely right," somebody said.

"That's why I think we've already done more than enough with this Poor Relief business. *Noblesse oblige* is all very well, but what man in his right mind hands out food to his enemy? We've been feeding most of the country for the last two years, and they are still plotting against us."

There was a murmur of agreement.

Elizabeth felt sick to her stomach. Although by now she knew that her father thought like that, it hurt to hear him say it.

Chapter 15

The shoot ended, the guests left and the castle lapsed into its normal routine. Lady Roscawl took to her bed, complaining of exhaustion after all the work she had done to entertain the visitors. Still confined indoors, Elizabeth spent most of her time in the library reading or pacing the corridors to try to work off some of her energy.

"You're going to marry a mummy's boy, I hear," William said to her one day. It was the first time that he had spoken to her for weeks.

Elizabeth did not reply, she just glared at him.

"At least we'll be rid of you."

"Go to hell, William." She had never sworn before, but she could not help herself.

"You're the one who's heading that way, Elizabeth."

From the look in his eyes, she knew that he was enjoying taunting her. She ignored his last remark and went up to her room, slamming the door behind her. He could not follow her there.

If only he knew that she planned to run away with Michael, that her wedding to Edward Cavendish would never take place. The only trouble was that Elizabeth hated deceit; she hated pretence of any sort, although she knew that she did not have any choice.

Thinking back to the spring, she remembered Sarah's wedding. Lord Homerton and her father were friends and colleagues at the House of Lords; she supposed they had worked out the match between them. Certainly Sarah had never laid eyes upon Johnny Homerton before he turned up at a shoot, but the difference was that she had liked him instantly. Sarah wanted to get married so that she could take her place in society; unlike Elizabeth, she did not question her way of life.

For a while, Elizabeth wondered what Sarah would have done if she had not liked Johnny, but she could not imagine her sister going against the wishes of her parents. She was glad that her sister's marriage seemed to be a happy one.

The weather had changed; a soft rain was falling. She went to the window and looked down to the stable yard and then beyond that to the rolling hills. A mile or two away, Michael would be hard at work on the roads. The thought of him brought a smile to her face; it would not be so long now.

A line of girls walked out of the yard, taking the track towards the village. Each of them was carrying a sack; they looked unhappy, though Elizabeth did not know why. Now that the shoot was over, the girls who had been taken on to help had been discharged. She thought they would have been glad of the chance of even a little work.

Eithne came in with a bundle of freshly laundered underwear, which she began to put away in a chest of drawers.

"The girls looked upset," Elizabeth said.

"Aye, Miss Elizabeth. They're not too pleased because they got paid in kind."

"What's that?"

"They got paid in meal and some cheese instead of money."

"What about the beaters? Did they get paid in meal as well?"

"I don't know. I suppose so."

Elizabeth's heart sank. She knew that Michael had been relying on money from the shoot to pay his fare to Liverpool. Eithne caught the look on her face.

"Is there anything the matter, Miss Elizabeth?"

"No," she said quickly. She did not want to burden the maid with her troubles, though she needed to get a message to Michael. "Could you ask Jamie to take a message to the village, Eithne?"

The maid had finished putting the underwear away. She stood up. "Jamie's gone, Miss Elizabeth. I thought you knew."

"Gone. Why?"

"He got the sack. They blamed him for letting you take the cart to the village."

The knowledge shot a bolt of guilt through Elizabeth.

"Don't worry," Eithne said, "he's a bright lad. He'll manage, if anyone can."

Although Elizabeth smiled, she felt pain inside. She had wanted to do good, but all she had done was to cause harm.

Lunch was an uncomfortable meal. Lady Roscawl was still in bed, and Elizabeth's brothers and father talked about estate matters as if she was not there. Once, she tried to join the conversation with a comment, but they ignored her, acting as if she had not spoken. Afterwards, she went to the library, where she began to flick through a copy of *Punch*; the cartoons always amused her.

Heavy footsteps disturbed her a short while later. The door was slightly ajar; she looked up and saw the factor pass by on his way to her father's study. Elizabeth waited for a moment, then she got up and followed him.

Carefully, she looked around, but there was nobody to see her. Raucous laughter came from the smoking-room, where her brothers were playing cards. Like a mouse, she crept along the corridor until she was outside the study.

Listening through the door, Elizabeth heard them talking about the shoot. Her father thanked Fraser for making sure it had gone so smoothly. The bag had been excellent. They chatted jovially for a while then, to end the conversation, her father said that he trusted that there were no problems.

"There is just one small thing," Fraser said. "I've decided to evict a tenant from Roscawl."

"Why's that? I thought the rents were paid."

"The rents are paid, right enough, but there's still arrears outstanding. There's one lad who's been causing a bit of trouble. I think we're best to get rid of him."

"Trouble? What kind of trouble? I thought that Young Ireland nonsense was over. I won't tolerate any of that on the estate."

"It's not that, Milord. No, this lad, O'Shea's his name, he set out to waylay a merchant by the name of O'Callaghan, would have robbed him but fortunately O'Callaghan's men were able to defend him. He's a troublemaker for sure. You're best to be rid of him. Besides, an eviction will keep the rest of them in line."

"Very well, Fraser. I'll leave it up to you," her father said.

Elizabeth slipped away, fear gnawing at the pit of her stomach. Michael had not tried to rob O'Callaghan, he had simply tried to get a fair price for the oats; he had told her all about it. She had to get word to him quickly, warn him what was going on.

Then, with sickening certainty, she realized that with his family facing eviction, Michael would not leave for Liverpool, even if he somehow found the fare. He would have to stay and care for them as best he could.

What on earth was she going to do?

Suddenly, Edward Cavendish's face floated before her. With a sickening certainty, she knew that if she did not do something, she would be forced to marry him and Michael's family would be evicted; that, whatever she did, Michael's family would be evicted anyway.

All afternoon she thought, but no good ideas came into her mind. Panic-stricken, she found it difficult to reason clearly. For a long time, she gazed out of her window at the land that she loved; its gentle beauty gave her a little comfort. Finally, she gathered herself together, decided to try to talk to her father. If he did not insist upon her marrying Edward Cavendish, then at least one of her worries would be over – and she would have more time to do something to help Michael.

He looked at her coldly when she knocked at the door of his study and then asked him if she could talk to him.

"I don't have much time, Elizabeth. I'm very busy."

She took a breath. "Edward Cavendish asked me to marry him."

"So your mother told me."

Elizabeth gulped. "Father, I don't want to marry him."

Lord Roscawl frowned. "It's a bit late to change your mind. Your mother told me you had already accepted."

"Only because she forced me too."

"Elizabeth, really…"

"Do I have to marry him?" she blurted.

"Your mother's of the opinion, and I agree, that it's in your best interests if you settle down. She's planning to leave for London soon. If you back down on your promise to marry the young Cavendish, then you'll cause us all a great deal of embarrassment. Then again, you seem to enjoy causing us embarrassment. Don't you?" He waited for her reply.

"No, I don't," she said, stiffly. She could tell by his attitude that he had little or no sympathy for her.

"The young Cavendish is a good match, a far better match than you've a right to expect. Of course, I cannot force you to marry him, but, if you've any sense, you will. Your mother and I both feel that it is the right thing to do. Any sensible girl would listen to the advice of her parents."

"Yes, Father," she said, meekly.

It did not matter, she thought. Whatever happened, whatever her parents did, she would never marry Edward Cavendish. Though she had expected her father's disinterest, it hurt to know that he did not care for her feelings.

The plan came to her that night, as she lay awake watching the passage of the moon over the velvety black Irish sky. It was not perfect, and it was risky but, with luck, it would work. The more she thought about it, the more she became sure that it would work. It had to; she had no other choice.

In the morning, she waited until her brothers had gone out for a ride and her father was working in his study, then she walked along to the gunroom at the end of the corridor. She had only been in the room once or twice before; she did not like guns, hated the sound that they made. The racks of rifles and muskets made her shiver. In a drawer, she found what she was looking for, a pair of percussion pistols made by Staudenmeyer of London.

One day a couple of years ago, before he had gone to Oxford, Albert had taken these pistols out to practise shooting pigeons. Although Elizabeth hated the idea of killing anything, she had been curious to know how the guns worked and Albert had shown her. The mechanism was simple, she had just to put a pellet in the chamber and load a percussion cap and then it was ready to fire.

The gun was heavy, it was difficult to hold it straight, but she had some time to practise. She took both pistols, a handful of pellets and two packets of percussion caps, which she bundled into a pillow case and carried upstairs to her bedroom, where she hid them in the bottom of her chest.

The next part of her plan was easier. Elizabeth went to the storeroom beyond the bedrooms where her brothers' old clothes were kept, and found a pair of trousers, a shirt and a jacket that fitted her. In the cloakroom downstairs she found an old cap that her father sometimes wore when he went stalking; he would not miss it. Back in her bedroom, she tried the clothes on and looked at her reflection in the mirror. From a distance, she thought, she could pass as a man. She would have to cover her face with a scarf.

She spent the rest of the day practising holding the pistol. By dinnertime, she could hold it in one hand without it wavering.

It would do, she thought. She had no intention of firing it.

Eithne brought her tea on Sunday morning. Elizabeth looked at the maid, puzzled. Usually, she went to early mass and one of the kitchen maids brought her tea. The maid smiled at her then opened her wardrobe and began to take clothes out.

"Aren't you going to church?" Elizabeth asked her.

"I doubt I'll have time," Eithne replied. "The Lord will have to forgive me missing it for once."

"Why not?"

Eithne turned to her. "Didn't your mother tell you?"

"Tell me what?"

"You're going to London tomorrow. I've got to get you all packed and ready."

Elizabeth sat up in bed, shocked. Her mother had said nothing to her; in fact, she had not seen her since the shoot because she'd been in bed.

"I thought she wasn't well," she said.

"She must be feeling better. She told Brigid last night. I thought you knew all about it."

Elizabeth got up and dressed quickly, wondering what on earth to do. She had thought she had a week or more to put her plan into action; she had no idea that her mother was intending to leave so soon.

After breakfast, she went with her brothers and father to the service in the Church of Ireland chapel in the castle grounds. It was the only time in the week that she was allowed to go out of doors, and usually she relished the short walk for the brief breath of fresh air, but today she hardly noticed it.

The sermon was short; her father disliked long theological monologues and the minister who came from Kilkenny knew that. Elizabeth did not notice that the service was over until her father rose to leave; she was too busy thinking.

Back at the castle, Eithne was nearly finished packing.

"I'm not feeling very well," Elizabeth said. "I think I'll lie down for a bit."

The maid looked concerned. "Are you sickening for something, Miss Elizabeth?"

"No, Eithne. It's just that time of the month, you know." It was not, but the maid accepted the lie.

"I'll just warm the bed for you, Miss Elizabeth."

The maid's concern made her feel guilty. "No," she said, "don't bother. I'll be fine once I've had a nap."

"Shall I wake you for dinner?"

"No. I haven't been sleeping well, I'm very tired. I'll ring if I need you."

The maid smiled and left. Elizabeth listened to her fading footsteps, then murmured a brief prayer. There was no choice; if she wanted to run away, she had to go now.

Chapter 16

Taking the spare pillows from the linen chest at the foot of her bed, Elizabeth bundled them into the bedclothes and then drew the covers up to make it look as if she was sleeping. Then she took her dress off and put on the clothes she had taken from the store cupboard. Looking at her reflection in the mirror, she put the cap on so that it covered her hair, then she took a long plain silk scarf from her drawer and wrapped it around her face. The image that faced her was anonymous: nobody would know it was her and she was tall enough to pass as a man.

Taking the pistols from their hiding place, she put one in each of the large pockets of the jacket. She carried the pellets and percussion caps separately; she knew that it was very dangerous to carry a loaded gun.

Finally she put on her riding boots, rolling the trouser legs down over them so that the expensive burnished leather was hidden.

It was a strange feeling, to look around her room, with all its familiar things, and know that she would never see it again if her plan succeeded, to know that she would never see it again even if she failed, because the wrath of her parents would be too terrible to contemplate. The castle had been her home for all of her life; she smiled to herself, remembering the games of hide and seek that she had played in the corridors when she was little. It was in this room that Nanny O'Dwyer had cared for her and loved her and told her all the wonderful bedtime stories that she still remembered now.

Thinking of her beloved nanny, Elizabeth wondered what the old lady would say if she knew what she planned to do now. For the first time, she was glad that Nanny O'Dwyer had died when she did, before the potato blight and the terrible hunger that came with it. The devastation and the disease would have broken the old lady's gentle heart.

The ringing of the lunch bell interrupted Elizabeth's thoughts. There was no more time to dither, she had to go now when her family was in the dining-room and the servants busy seeing to them.

For one final time, she looked around her. She was not sorry to leave, but fleetingly she thought of Eithne, of what would happen to her maid when it was discovered that she had gone. The thought of Eithne being sacked concerned her, the fate of Jamie still nagged at her conscience, but there was nothing she could do.

Murmuring a prayer, she opened the window, climbed out, hung from the ledge as Michael had done and then dropped to the ground. The impact sent a sharp pain up her legs, she paused for a moment to regain her breath, then strode quickly across the yard and through the gate. The sound of her boots striking the gravel seemed very loud to her, she was afraid that someone would hear her, but when she listened there was no sound beyond the barking of one of the dogs.

Elizabeth set off over the fields. At the top of the rise, she turned and looked back at the castle; when she saw nobody following her, she walked on.

The factor's house came into view. Behind a stone dyke, Elizabeth stopped, took one of the guns out of her pocket and loaded it carefully. The yard outside the house was empty; that meant he had no visitors. She was pleased about that. If there had been any visitors, she would have had to wait until they were gone.

Slowly, making as little noise as possible, she walked up to the front door and knocked. The maid would answer, she thought; she had planned for that, regretted the fact that she would have to tie the girl up.

No answer came. After waiting for a minute or two, Elizabeth knocked again, but there was still no answer.

Gingerly, she turned the door knob. The door swung open.

Elizabeth paused; that had not been her plan. She had expected the maid to answer the door and tell her where the factor was. The pistol was in her right hand, its weight dragging at her arm.

She walked along the hallway; she tried the study door, but it was locked. The door on the other side opened on a dining-room, which was empty. The factor had to be here, she thought. Although the maid must have been given time off, the house would surely have been locked if he was away too.

The next door opened on a small drawing-room, in which a fire blazed brightly. Fraser was in a chair by the fireside, snoring gently. On a table beside him, there was a decanter and a half-filled glass.

"Wake up," Elizabeth said. When nothing happened, she said it again, loudly this time. The factor stirred, but his eyes did not open.

She picked up the decanter, poured the contents over him.

Fraser spluttered into wakefulness. "What the hell…"

Elizabeth was aiming the gun directly at him. "Don't move," she said, in a gruff, low voice. "Put your hands up."

"What the blazes?"

"Put your hands up," she yelled.

He complied slowly. She realized that he was a little drunk.

"Now wait a minute…"

"Silence!" she roared.

He trembled at the tone of her voice. His expression changed from shock to one of fear. "Please," he said.

"Hands up," she said, sharply.

He raised his hands. "Please," he whined, "I'm just the factor, I'm just doing my job. I just do the Lord's bidding."

"Shut up!" she said. "You stole money from the priest."

"I did not."

"You took fifteen pounds from him which was meant to go to the rents, but you kept it for yourself. I want it back."

"Yes," he whimpered. "I'll give you it. It's in the cash box in the study. Please, for the sake of God, don't kill me."

"Stand up," she said, "slowly now. Keep your hands above your head." She waited for him to obey her. "Now, where's the key to the study?"

"On the t-table," he replied, stuttering with fear.

She looked down and saw it. Keeping the gun pointing at him, she reached for it with her left hand and picked it up.

"Now," she said, "walk to the study. Slowly mind, keep your hands above your head." It was difficult to keep her voice low and gruff; she had to concentrate.

Fraser did as she told him, quaking with fear. At the study door, she put the key in the lock. It was stiff, hard to turn, doubly difficult because she could only use her left hand. From reading Albert's adventure stories, Elizabeth knew that it was important to make the factor keep his hands where she could see them. If he had the slightest chance to overpower her, he would not hesitate to do so.

She struggled with the key in the lock. Finally it turned and she gestured to him to go inside.

"Where's the money?"

"In the cash box. The bottom drawer of the desk."

She tried the drawer, found that it was locked.

"K-key's under the paperweight."

Elizabeth found the key, opened the drawer. As she reached for the box, the factor lunged for her. Automatically, her finger tightened on the trigger. The gun fired, a loud crack that astonished both of them. Fraser fell to the floor, whimpering. Elizabeth recovered first. She reached into her other pocket and took the second gun, which she pointed at him.

The shot was wild, it had lodged in the ceiling, missing the factor by a mile.

"Next time," she bluffed, "I'll shoot to kill." Only she knew that the gun was not even loaded. She waited until the factor was on his feet with his arms above his head, then she opened the box. It was filled with paper money and coins.

"Take it," Fraser whined. "Take it all."

Elizabeth had never seen paper money before, she had only seen the coins that her father had given her. For a moment, she looked at the notes, then she took one marked Ten Pounds Sterling, another marked Five Pounds Sterling, which she stuffed into her trouser pocket.

"I only want what you stole," she said.

"Please," he whimpered, "I beg you, don't kill me. I was going to put the money to the rents. Truly, I was."

"Shut up!" She moved aside, gestured that he should sit down at the desk. "Now," she said, "you're going to write out a confession."

"W-what?"

"A confession, Fraser. Write that Father O'Shaughnessy gave you £15 two months ago and you didn't credit it to the rents."

"But I told you, I was going to."

Elizabeth pointed the gun at him. "I'm warning you…"

Reluctantly, he picked up a pen, inked it and began to write. When he was finished, she read what he had written then told him to blot it. Once the ink was quite dry, she folded the letter with one hand, keeping the gun trained on him with the other, and put it in her pocket.

"P-please," he stammered, "d-don't kill me. I was going to pay the money to the rents, as God's my judge."

"Don't tempt me," she said, coldly.

Impatiently, she motioned him towards the kitchen. There, she found that his pantry locked; she had thought that she would leave him in the cellar with furniture piled on top of the trapdoor, but the pantry was better. Once he was inside and the door was locked, she pocketed the key.

"Fraser," she said, through the door. "I'm not one of your tenants, so I'm not afraid of you. But I will be watching you. Any more trickery against the tenants, and I'll be back. Next time, I won't be so gentle. Do you understand?"

His answer was a muffled "Yes".

In the stables, Elizabeth put the bridle on the factor's colt. There was another colt and an old mare. Mounting the colt, she drove the other horses out of the stables and along the track for a bit and then she set them free.

It was a beautiful day, the sun shone from a cloudless sky and there was just enough of a breeze to cool her flushed cheeks.

Elizabeth was exhilarated that her plan had worked. She had not expected it to be so easy; but in a way she was not surprised that the factor had turned out to be a coward.

For a moment, she wondered if she should have taken more money, but she did not want to steal, she just wanted to take back what the factor had stolen. Michael would be pleased, she thought, as she rode towards the village. They would have plenty of money now to get to Liverpool.

Chapter 17

Michael was pacing the cottage, from wall to wall. For hours now, he had been talking to his mother, pleading with her, eventually arguing, but she would not agree.

"For pity's sake," he said, "I'm not a boy any longer. I'm twenty years old. I'm a man."

"You're still my son," she said, adamantly. "And no son of mine is leaving this house without a penny in his pocket. Don't you know how many beggars there are on the streets? There's no work, not anywhere in Ireland."

"I'd manage."

"You're not taking the risk."

When the boys had come back from the shoot with meal but no money, he had decided to leave for Liverpool anyway. Although he had no money, he thought that he would find work somewhere, manage somehow. Maybe he could work his passage over on the boat, he had heard of others doing that.

He remembered his promise to Elizabeth; he did not want to break it.

The only thing that he was sure of was that there was no hope at home, no hope in all of Ireland.

"You can't stop me," he said, anger in his voice.

Although he loved his mother dearly, sometimes he thought she was a little too concerned for him.

She sat down tiredly. "No, I suppose not. But I'll not give you my blessing."

He sat down too. A look passed between them; they both knew that Michael would not leave against his mother's wishes.

"You worry too much."

"Maybe, Michael. But the streets are full of beggars, and there's fever in the cities, worse than fever's ever been here. I trust you, of course, but I don't want you to take the risk."

"But there's nothing here, Ma. Only a half pound of grain a day from the roads. They'd stop that too, if they could. The only chance we've got is if I can get away." It hurt him to say that, because he loved his country.

"I know, Michael, but bear with me, please. If you went away without money, I'd worry so. Just wait, through the winter at least. Who knows what tomorrow will bring?"

Michael shook his head. They both knew it would take a miracle.

Liam ran through the cottage door. "Michael, Ma, Elizabeth's here, the girl from the castle."

Shyly, she followed him in. Not wanting to be seen, she had gone beyond the village and left the horse tied to a gate, then she had walked back.

Michael took in her clothes, the cap that covered her hair. "Elizabeth. What on earth?"

"Nobody knows I'm gone, yet," she said.

Mary O'Shea stood up, smiling. She knew that it was

Elizabeth who had left the food. "You're very welcome, dear," she said. "I've little to offer you but a cup of herb tea."

Elizabeth took the stool she offered. Quickly, she told Michael what she had done, that she had taken back the money the factor had stolen from the priest. Then she told him of Fraser's plans to evict him and his family, that when she'd heard that she knew that she had to do something. "But it doesn't matter," she finished, "I've plenty of money to take us all to Liverpool."

Michael stood up, began to pace the cottage again. Mary O'Shea stirred the brew of herbal tea, then poured a cup, which she handed to Elizabeth. Although her expression was serious, she said nothing.

Michael did not speak while Elizabeth drank the tea. It had a pleasant, almost sweet taste.

"Michael," she said, when she finished it. "Aren't you pleased?"

He turned round and faced her, smiling sadly. He was filled with a mixture of emotions: anger, rage at Fraser, exasperation with her for not discussing her plans with him.

"I wished you'd talked to me first," he said.

"There was no time," she replied. "Last week, when I heard about the beaters, I knew I had to do something. I thought I had some time. I was going to ask Eithne to give you a message. Then I found out today that my mother was planning to leave for London tomorrow. I had to act then. I didn't do anything wrong."

Michael opened his mouth to say something, but his mother held up her hand to stop him. "I know you didn't do anything wrong, Elizabeth," she said. "I know, Michael knows, surely God knows too. But that's not the way it'll be seen."

"Fraser can't complain," Elizabeth said quickly, reaching into her pocket. "Look. I made him sign a confession."

Michael glanced at the paper. "You left him locked in the pantry."

"I had to."

"I know, *mavourneen*. But he's got to explain that. If I know anything about him, I know that he'll hide the rest of the money, and say that it's all been stolen. Soon's he's found, they'll be out looking for the robbers. And they won't be looking for you. Most likely, I'll get the blame."

Elizabeth's face fell. "But the confession. Won't it help?"

Michael shrugged. "He'll just say the robber forced him to write it. He'll still deny it."

Mary O'Shea looked from her son to Elizabeth, then back at Michael. For a while, her mother's instinct had been telling her that Michael had met a girl, but she had not known who. All she had known was that with the hunger there was nothing he could do about it and she had wished that times were different. Looking at Elizabeth, she knew that there could be no peace for them in Ireland, nor in England either.

"Listen to me," she said. They both looked at her. "Soon, they'll be out looking for you, the pair of you once they realize that Elizabeth's gone from the castle. Only God knows what they'd do if they caught you. We can't take the risk of that. We'd not be safe in Liverpool, we'd always be looking over our shoulders, afraid of being caught. You take the money, Michael, and go to America.

Take Elizabeth with you. Once you're there, you'll find work and you can send us our passage."

"But we can't leave you," Elizabeth said. "Not if you're going to be evicted."

"You don't know for sure," Mary O'Shea said. "If Michael's gone, we might not be evicted. Even if we are, we can go to my brother-in-law in Cork. It won't be for ever. There'll be a roof over our heads and we'll be fed. It's better than the risk of the pair of you going to jail or worse."

At the mention of America, Michael's spirits lifted, but he did not want his dream to come true at the expense of his family.

"Don't you see," his mother said, "it's the only thing to do, the only chance we've got? It's a free country over there, Michael. You're clever, you could make something of yourself. Heaven knows, in Liverpool, you'd only ever be a labourer, no more than that."

Michael looked at his mother, and then at Elizabeth. "I swear to God, Mother," he said, "I'll send the money for your passage as soon as I can. And Elizabeth, I'll marry you, if you'll have me. I'll make a good life for us all."

Elizabeth blushed with pleasure. He was looking at her intently. "Will you marry me, Elizabeth?"

"Yes," she said. "Of course. Of course I will, Michael." If there was any certainty in her life, it was the knowledge that she loved him.

Mary O'Shea smiled at her. "It's a hard life you've chosen, pet, but he's a good man, I promise you that."

"I know that."

"Look at you," Mary said. "I've a spare skirt and blouse

I hid from the officers, a shawl too that you can have."

Elizabeth did not understand what she meant.

"The Poor Law Relieving Officers," Mary said. "Before you get work on the roads, they come to your house to check you're destitute. You're only allowed the clothes you stand up in, you see, and bedding and that. Anything else, you're expected to sell."

The shock showed on Elizabeth's face.

"Don't worry, pet," Mary said. "It'll soon be over, once we're in America."

"I'll leave you a letter to my father," Elizabeth said. "I'll tell him that it was me who robbed Fraser, and nobody else. And that I didn't rob him really."

"No," Michael said, "we'll go to the priest, talk to him. With Fraser's confession, maybe he can talk to your father." He turned to Liam. "Go and take the factor's horse. Try and get the others on the way. Ride towards Kilkenny and then let them go somewhere they'll be found. It might lead them off our track."

The priest listened in silence to Elizabeth's story, then he smiled at her. "I won't say that what you did was right, but it certainly was not wrong."

"I had to do something," she said.

"And now you're headed for America?"

She nodded. "Unless you want the money back. Remember, I gave it to you."

"No, child. It'd do more good if it could get the two of you to America." He gave her some paper and a pen.

Dear Father, she wrote.

This is to let you know that I will not be coming back

to the castle. I cannot bear to contemplate marriage to Edward Cavendish and I know that if I did not marry him you would just expect me to marry someone else like him. I also feel that it is wrong to live the way you live in the castle, with so much, while so many others are living on the verge of starvation.

This afternoon, I went to the factor's house. Using pistols which I took from the gunroom at the castle, I forced him to return to me money that he had, in effect, stolen from the priest, Father O'Shaughnessy. Some time ago, I gave Father O'Shaughnessy my gold locket, which he sold for £15. He gave the money to the factor to go towards the rents, because at the time we feared you would evict the tenants. Fraser did not credit the money in the rent book, though, he kept it for himself. Here is a confession that he wrote and signed himself. The rents were paid with money from the oats.

I left Fraser locked in the kitchen pantry. I dressed in old clothes belonging to Albert. If Fraser claims that more than £15 was taken, do not believe him. I am returning with Father O'Shaughnessy the pistols I took from the gunroom.

Please do not blame him, or anyone else, for my actions, which are mine and mine alone.

Your daughter Elizabeth.

Once she had finished writing, she blotted the letter carefully and handed it to the priest. "Will it do?"

"I can but try. The confession will help. Will your father recognize your writing?"

"I don't know." She had never had reason to write to

him before. She took the guns from her pocket and handed them to him. "He will recognize these, though."

Gingerly, the priest picked up one of the pistols. "It's not loaded?"

"No." She gave him the pellets and the packet of percussion caps.

"You know, these guns are valuable."

"I don't want to take anything that isn't mine," she said. Michael nodded vigorously.

"Bless you, child," he said. "God bless the pair of you."

Father O'Shaughnessy wrote a letter of introduction for them; he gave Michael his baptismal certificate and a certificate identifying Elizabeth, which they would need in America.

Michael's mother was waiting for them outside his house. She gave Elizabeth a bundle of clothes and pushed a package into Michael's hands. Michael looked, saw that it was a scone which she had made with the flour gathered from the dregs of the wheat harvest and a precious egg, and some of the smoked trout that he had poached.

"I don't need it," he said. "I can always guddle a fish on the way."

"For the journey," she told him.

They embraced, holding each other for a long time. Elizabeth saw tears in Michael's eyes, and tears came into her own.

When they let each other go, Mary O'Shea took Elizabeth's hands.

"I'll pray for you," she said.

"It won't be long, Mother," Michael said.

"God bless, son."

Chapter 18

They set off, over the fields, avoiding the roads in case patrols were already out looking for them. When they reached the hill above the village, Michael stopped and looked back at the ramshackle little houses. Roscawl was not much, but it had been his home for all of his life and he knew that he would miss the beauty of the land and the big Irish sky.

They were heading for Cork, more than fifty miles away, where they could get a boat to America.

"You're very quiet," Elizabeth said, after a while.

Michael frowned. "I'm a bit ashamed, if you want to know."

"Ashamed. Why?"

"Because you took a terrible risk going to Fraser. You were dead lucky that he was drunk. If he hadn't been, you wouldn't have got away with it. He would have caught you somehow, and God knows what your father would have done."

Elizabeth shivered at the thought of it.

"I should have done it," Michael continued. "I should've helped you. I'm ashamed that I didn't."

"How could you? You didn't know."

Michael stopped then, held a finger to his lips. Very far

away, Elizabeth heard the sound of a horse's hooves. There was a rock nearby; they hid behind it. The sound faded.

"If you ever need to take a risk again, Elizabeth, will you tell me about it?"

"Yes," she said.

For an hour, they walked on. Michael kept up a fast pace. Elizabeth, who was not so used to walking, had to work hard to keep up. Again, they heard the sound of a horse and again Michael insisted they hide.

"They probably don't even know I'm gone, yet," she said, when the sound had faded.

"The factor's maid'll be back by now. She'll have found him, and he'll go straight to the castle. Maybe they don't know you're gone, but they'll be out soon looking for a robber wearing the clothes you're wearing, if they're not out now."

She looked down at her jacket and trousers. "Should I change?"

"No, *mavourneen*, it's better to keep off the roads. I don't want us to be seen. You can change when we get to Cork. We can probably get a shilling or two for these clothes there."

Far to the west, the sun was low in the sky. Its rays were strong, casting auburn highlights through Michael's hair. Elizabeth felt a thrill when she looked at him, knowing now that she could spend the rest of her life with him. It was all she had ever wanted, to be with him. As a boy, he had been her hero; her love for him had grown out of that childish attraction.

"When my father gets my letter, they won't be looking for a robber."

"No," Michael replied, "they'll be looking for you."

After the sun set, as dusk spread over the land, they stopped at a stream for a drink of water. Elizabeth had never drunk without a cup, Michael had to show her how to use her hands. The cool water slaked her thirst. Carefully, Michael divided the scone into quarters, giving her one, taking one himself, and keeping the rest for later.

"I think we should walk through the night, if you can," he said. "Then we'll find a place to rest through the day. I want to get as far away from Roscawl as we can before we stop."

Elizabeth agreed, although her feet were beginning to hurt. "How long will it take us to get to Cork?"

Michael smiled. He was used to walking long distances, he could manage fifty miles easily in a day but he knew that she could not. "Maybe two days, maybe a bit less. Depends how fast we go."

He took her hand, she felt a thrill.

The moon rose, the sky was dusted by stars. It was after dinner time. Fleetingly, Elizabeth thought of the food that would be served in the castle, felt a pang of hunger. By now, they would know that she was gone. In her mind's eye, she saw her father, stern faced. It would take time to organize a search party; they would have to send to Kilkenny for constables or soldiers to help.

Michael squeezed her hand, they walked on. Reaching a small river, he picked her up and carried her across so that her boots would not get wet.

"It'll probably be tomorrow before they start looking for us," she said. The pain in her feet was getting worse.

"Maybe."

Thinking about her letter, she realized that it would not stop her father searching for her. Her defiance would only make him angrier.

Michael began to whistle a tune, then he stopped. Lord Roscawl's wrath would be terrible if they were caught; he had to stay alert, listen to any sounds of pursuit. Although he had done nothing wrong, he would be blamed; if they were caught, he would probably be accused of kidnapping Elizabeth. For a moment, he felt exasperated with her for not talking to him first, discussing her ideas with him, then he realized that she did the only thing that could have been done. If she had done nothing, he would have been stuck in Roscawl and she would have been forced to marry a man that she did not love.

In the light of the moon her hair shone silvery-gold; he felt a rush of love for her, for her bravery and her kindness. He wished that things were different, though, that she did not have to take the risk that she had.

In America, he vowed, things would be different. There was work there, the chance for a man to make something of himself. He would work hard, make a good life for them both, for his family as well. All he needed was an opportunity, he could do the rest.

The moon passed behind a cloud. It was very dark and a chill wind was blowing from the east. They were in County Tipperary now, heading south-west. In the distance, Michael saw a village; when they got closer, he realized that it was unoccupied, the people evicted. The roofs were burnt, only the walls still stood. It was a sad place, he could almost feel the anguish of the people who had once lived there.

He shuddered and walked on.

Elizabeth was getting tired, he sensed she was struggling to keep up. He turned to her. "We could stop for a bit, *mavourneen*, if you like."

"No," she smiled bravely. "I'm fine."

It began to rain, a fine drizzle that matted the hair on his head. The grass became damp and slippery underfoot. There was a hill before them; Michael was anxious to get to the top, to see if he could see the Comeragh mountains in the distance. The mountains were twenty miles away from Roscawl; he wanted to reach them by the time they stopped in the morning. Once they were there, he would feel safe from any search parties that Lord Roscawl sent out. There were plenty of hiding places amongst the rocks.

Beside him, Elizabeth slipped on the wet grass, crying out in surprise. Although his hand tightened on hers she fell awkwardly, twisting her ankle.

"Are you all right, *mavourneen*?" he asked anxiously.

She smiled. "Yes."

She got up slowly. He saw the pain on her face as she put her weight on the injured ankle. Inadvertently, she yelped.

His heart sank. "It's my fault," he said. "I was going too fast."

Elizabeth gritted her teeth. The pain was severe, but she had to walk, somehow. She took one step, then another, then the agony forced her to stop.

"I'm sorry," she said.

He squatted down, told her to climb on his back. She did as he said. He picked her up and carried her to the top of the hill. From there, he could not see the mountains, but he did see a wood, where he thought they could hide for a while.

It took a long time to reach the wood. When at last they were under the shelter of trees, Michael put Elizabeth down. He found a log for her to sit on, then he took off her riding boot and gently examined her ankle. Although it was swollen and bruised, he could feel no broken bones. He was thankful for that.

"You'll live," he said.

She smiled wanly. "We should've taken Fraser's horse."

Michael shook his head. "I don't think so. It's a good horse, anybody can see that. With me in these clothes, it would be obvious we'd stolen it."

"Yes, but we'd have been in Cork by the morning. We could have left it just outside the city."

"It doesn't matter now, *mavourneen*." He put his arm around her. "Hush now. Try to get some sleep."

"My ankle should be better in the morning."

"Yes," he said, though he knew that a sprain like that took a week at least to heal.

As Elizabeth slept, he sat awake thinking. By now, he was sure that they would know that she was gone; they would already be out looking. They would find the horses on the way to Kilkenny – he hoped that would delay them a bit, lead them in the wrong direction. Soon, though, they would find that he and Elizabeth had not passed through the town, then they would fan out and search in all directions. Though he and Elizabeth had covered twelve miles, maybe more, that lead was nothing to men on horseback.

In the chill of the night, he shivered and hugged her

tightly to him. Her soft breathing lulled him and soon he fell asleep too.

A few hours later, he woke up suddenly. He did not know what had disturbed him, but he was angry with himself because he had not meant to sleep. For a moment, he listened, hearing nothing and then, far away, he heard the sound of horses.

Elizabeth was still sleeping beside him. He shook her to wake her, then held his finger to his lips.

"What?" she murmured.

"Ssshh. I think they're coming."

This time, they both heard the horses. Elizabeth got up and tried to walk, but the pain in her ankle was excruciating; she could not move.

He picked her up in his arms and walked deeper into the woods, looking for a hiding place.

"Michael," she said, "you go. Run! They don't know you're with me."

"Ssshhh," he said. "Don't you dare even suggest it."

Elizabeth felt heartsick at the thought that they might be caught. She could not bear the thought of anything happening to Michael. If she was caught, the worst her father could do would be to keep her confined to the castle, but he would have Michael prosecuted, she was sure; for what, she did not know.

The sound of horses was coming closer. Now, they could hear dogs baying too. Michael looked around and saw a big, old oak tree, its branches covered by leaves.

"We'll have to climb it," he said, putting her down. "I'll go first." He climbed to the first branch, then reached for

Elizabeth. She handed him her bundle of clothes, then he lifted her up. Very slowly, branch by branch, they climbed the tree, until Michael thought they were high enough. Elizabeth did not have a good head for heights; she dared not look down.

The thick leaves hid them from view. There was a sound in the undergrowth, and a hound appeared directly underneath them, barking.

"Can it see us?" Elizabeth whispered.

"Ssshhh!" Michael hissed.

The hound barked some more and pawed at the ground. Michael whistled softly to it, then he took a piece of scone from his pocket and threw it. The hound dived after it, yelping gleefully.

The undergrowth was too thick for a man on horseback; they heard heavy footsteps, the sound of voices.

Elizabeth was almost too scared to breathe.

The hound came back, looked up hopefully. Michael threw it another bit of scone.

"Doesn't look like there's anyone here," a man's voice said.

"We'd better take a good look," another voice said, "to make sure."

Elizabeth closed her eyes; it was her brother William. She remembered his glee when the coachmen had been accused of theft and the way he'd mocked her. The two men were almost directly under the oak tree; through the leaves she could see that the other one was a soldier.

"She's been away all night," the soldier said, "chances are she'd have gone further than this."

"She's not hiding in the village, that's for sure," William said.

Beside her, she sensed Michael freeze. The hound was back again, whimpering hopefully. William and the soldier walked on a couple of paces. Michael threw a bit of fish to distract the hound; it flew after it.

"What's that?" William asked.

"The damned beast is chasing rabbits," the soldier replied. "Come on. There's nobody here. She doesn't have a horse?"

"No, I'm sure of that."

"There's a village a few miles south of here. Let's go and see if anyone's seen anything."

William stopped. "They're hardly likely to tell us."

"They will, if we offer a shilling or two."

Michael closed his eyes. He had been hoping that they would go deeper into the wood; if they did, he thought that there was a chance that he could go back and take their horses, if he was quick. Then he realized that Elizabeth could not keep up with him, that, if he left them stranded in the wood, he would have to leave her with them. He cursed under his breath.

William and the soldier walked away, the dog running after them. After a moment, they heard them riding away.

Elizabeth breathed deeply; she was trembling. "That was close," she said.

"They're away now. We'll be safe for a while."

Michael was thinking. With her ankle injured, Elizabeth could not walk to Cork and it would take him an awful long time to carry her there. Along the way, someone was bound to see them and if William was offering a reward, the chances were that the person would tell. Yet they were sure that Elizabeth did not have a horse; they were not looking for someone on horseback.

"What is it?" she asked him.

He thought a moment longer. "I'm going to get a horse," he said.

"Michael! You can't."

"I can, *mavourneen*. They're not looking for us between here and the castle. I can go back and get one from the stables. There's nobody there, likely. Everybody's out, looking for you."

"But what if you get caught?"

"Hush, *mavourneen*. Trust me. I won't get caught. It's the only thing we can do. You can't walk, with that ankle, and it'd take all week if I carried you."

"Michael…"

He kissed her softly on the cheek, then swiftly climbed down the tree. "You wait there, Elizabeth. You're perfectly safe. I'll only be a few hours. I'll be back by noon."

Elizabeth opened her mouth to argue, but she knew that there was nothing that she could say.

Chapter 19

After Michael left Elizabeth, he ran all the way back to Roscawl, pausing every so often to walk for a while and catch his breath. Skirting the village, his heart aching as he thought of his mother, he went directly to the castle. Just outside the stable yard he stopped and felt fear for the first time. The yard was full of soldiers, about half a dozen of them milling around.

He hid in the ditch behind the wall, cursing and wondering what to do next. He had been so sure that they would all be away looking for Elizabeth, that it would be easy to take a horse from the stables. Although he could hear voices, he was not close enough to hear exactly what they were saying.

His heart pounding, he waited. After a time, the yard gate opened and two of the soldiers rode out. Very slowly, he stood up and looked over the wall; the other soldiers were sitting on upturned barrels, eating bread and cheese.

Michael swore to himself and then began to think of what to do. Elizabeth was safe for a while, he knew; they would not return to the wood. It might be best to go back there and wait until her ankle healed. For food, he could guddle trout and build a fire to cook them.

They would still have to get to Cork, though the

journey would be even more risky because by then the whole country would be looking for them.

What he needed to do, he realized, was the unexpected. If they were sure that Elizabeth did not have a horse, he had to find a horse and escape them that way. Again, Michael looked over the wall; the soldiers had not moved. Silently, he crept away.

When he reached the road to Kilkenny, he thought of going there to see if he could find the horses that Liam had abandoned. But Liam had known that he wanted the horses to be found to confuse the search parties, so he would have left them in a place where they would have been easily seen.

It was a hot day. Michael paused to wipe the sweat from his brow. Looking up, he saw the sun was high in the sky; he knew that Elizabeth would begin to worry, because he should have been back by now. He had to find a horse somewhere, but the only horses for miles around belonged either to Fraser or the castle. The few tenants who'd had horses had, like his father, been forced to sell them.

The idea came to him suddenly. At first, he thought it was so ridiculous that it would never work, but when he thought about it, he realized that it might. Certainly, it was the only thing he could think of.

He turned round and walked quickly back to the castle. When he reached the gate to the stable yard, he opened it and then boldly walked in, nodding to the soldiers. Inside, his stomach was churning with fear; if the soldiers noticed anything amiss, then they would challenge him and the game would be up. Michael had reckoned that, because they did not know him, when they saw him they would simply assume he was an estate employee on some errand or another.

Time seemed to come to a halt, he could hear his heart beating wildly, but the soldiers hardly noticed him, they just kept on chatting.

Gulping, Michael headed for the stables. He was nearly there when one of the soldiers shouted at him.

"Hey, lad! Can you get us some more of that ale?" He was grinning and holding up a tankard.

Michael stopped dead, wishing that the ground would open up and swallow him.

The soldier stood up and walked over to him. Michael opened his mouth to tell him to ask at the kitchen, then he realized that would not do. Taking the tankard, he said that he would ask.

At the kitchen door, he knocked loudly, praying that Mrs Murphy would not answer, because she would be sure to recognize him.

His luck held. A maid answered, a girl he did not recognize.

"The soldiers are asking for more ale," he said.

She pursed her lips and turned away, coming back a moment later with a brimming jug.

Michael took it to the soldiers, who thanked him.

Quickly, he went into the stables, put the bridle on the brown mare that Elizabeth always rode and then walked out of the yard with her, taking a sack of oats with him for the horse to eat. The soldiers did not even notice him go.

Outside the yard, he stopped for a moment until his heartbeat returned to normal. He felt faint, light-headed, dizzy with relief. Then he mounted the horse and set out for the woods. Although they had walked there over the moors, he decided to take the road, because that way was quicker.

After he had travelled for two or three miles, Michael began to relax and enjoy the ride. The warm wind blew in his face. He was exultant that he had managed to get a horse and outwit the soldiers. In no time at all, he would be back with Elizabeth; if they rode through the night, they would be in Cork by the morning.

The road topped a slight rise then turned a corner; he was galloping now, careless of the noise he was making. They were not looking for someone on horseback, after all, and the sooner he was back with Elizabeth the better.

In the distance, he saw a party of three or four men on horseback. For a moment, he thought he would just ride past them, then he realized that they would stop and question him. There was a risk he might be recognized, if one of them was Fraser or one of his men. They would want to know what a lad from the village was doing with such a fine horse.

Michael looked around, but he saw nowhere to hide, except for a low dyke that ran along the side of the road. He looked towards the men, but they did not seem to have seen him yet. He urged the horse over the dyke, then dismounted and urged the horse to lie down. The mare looked at him with soft brown eyes, uncomprehending for a moment, before she obeyed. Michael held his breath until the men passed; they had not seen him, they would have stopped if they had.

Cautiously he rode on, over the moors. It was midafternoon now and he knew that Elizabeth would be terribly worried. The road dipped towards a coppice, he slowed down to a trot, but he could see nothing. He was almost out of the little wood when a voice yelled to him to halt.

Michael froze.

O'Callaghan, the gombeen-man, came out from behind a beech tree. He was pointing a gun at him. "Don't move, or I'll shoot," he said.

Michael did not move, but his eyes looked around, searching for the sidekicks who always accompanied the gombeen man.

"It's the O'Shea laddie, isn't it? You're the one who wanted the oats back, after I'd paid a fair price for them. What are you doing with a horse, laddie?"

Michael glared at him, but he said nothing. His attention was fixed on the gun in O'Callaghan's hand; he was wondering if he could somehow disarm him.

"Get off the horse, slowly now. Don't be trying any of your tricks."

Michael obeyed.

"I asked you a question, boy. What are you doing with a horse?"

"It's none of your business, O'Callaghan."

"I reckon it is. I reckon Mr Fraser would like to know, as well. You and I, we're going back to the castle. I think you've got some questions to answer."

The only weapon that Michael had was the sack of oats, which he was holding in his hand.

"Unless, that is, you make it worth my while to let you go."

The gombeen-man was leering at him. Michael knew then that he was suspected of robbing Fraser, despite Elizabeth's letter; also that the factor had complained of losing much more than £15.

"I don't know what you mean," he said slowly.

"I think you do, laddie. I think you know exactly what I mean."

There was only one thing that Michael knew: whatever he did, O'Callaghan would report what he had seen to the factor. He had to play for time.

"What would it be that would be worth your while to let me go?" he asked, seeing that the gombeen-man's horse was drinking from a nearby stream. That must have been the reason why he stopped.

"Oh, I don't know now. Let me think." The gombeen-man's eyes drifted skywards, for a moment, his attention wavered. That was the moment Michael had been waiting for. Swiftly, he raised his right arm, sending the sack of oats crashing against O'Callaghan. The shock of the blow, rather than its force, made the gombeen-man fall down. His elbow hit a rock and the gun clattered out of his hand. Michael fell on it and grabbed it before he had a chance to recover.

By the time that O'Callaghan dazedly opened his eyes, Michael had the gun trained on him.

"P-please, don't shoot me," he begged.

Michael smiled to himself, thinking of all of the things the gombeen-man had done over the years to the villagers, how he had cheated them out of money and carried tales to the factor.

He did not intend to shoot him, but he did not know

what to do with him.

"I'll make it worth your while," the gombeen-man spluttered.

"Shut up," Michael said. He had to think and O'Callaghan's pleadings filled him with a sense of revulsion. If he had not managed to overpower him, he knew that the gombeen-man would not have hesitated to turn him in to the factor and the soldiers. Yet he did not want to kill him, he did not want to have anyone's death on his conscience. That left him with a problem: as soon as he let O'Callaghan go, he would tell the search parties all he knew.

Michael thought for a moment, then he told him to mount his horse. Taking the rope from the saddle of the gombeen-man's horse, he tied his hands loosely, with enough slack that he could still hold the reins. Keeping the gun aimed at him, he mounted the other horse and told him to ride slowly.

Leaving the track, they headed over the moors. The wood where he had left Elizabeth was only a couple of miles away; Michael knew that he must not let the gombeen-man know where she was.

Just before they reached the wood, he stopped and told the gombeen-man to dismount. As O'Callaghan obeyed with difficulty, he jumped off his horse, keeping the gun aimed at him.

"Where's your money?" Michael asked him.

"All I've got's in my pocket. You can have it. You can have more, if you spare me."

Michael ignored him and carefully reached into the pocket he indicated, where he found a heavy purse. Slowly, with one hand, he opened it and looked inside. There were a few guineas and some coins. Briefly, he considered taking the money; O'Callaghan had robbed the village of their oats, after all, but then he realized that there was something better he could do with it. He did not want to take anything that was not his; by rights, the money belonged not to O'Callaghan but to the people he had swindled and he did not have time to give it back to them.

Deftly, he untied the rope that bound the gombeen-man's hands.

"Take off your clothes," he said.

"What?"

"I said, take off your clothes. Do it!"

O'Callaghan looked at him oddly and obeyed slowly. When he reached his underclothes, Michael told him to take them off as well.

"B-but…"

"Just do it," Michael said.

There was a flask of whisky in his saddle-bag. When O'Callaghan was completely naked, Michael told him to drink it.

"What, all of it?"

"Yes," Michael said. As the gombeen-man drank, he bundled his clothes together and stuffed them into the bag. Then he waited.

Once the gombeen-man had finished the whisky, he burped, then he swayed slightly. Michael smiled to himself; he wanted him to be drunk. The gombeen-man burped again, then sat down with a surprised and stupid expression on his face.

Michael mounted his horse and took the reins of the

other one. He no longer needed to keep the gun trained on O'Callaghan. Taking the purse, he flung its contents wide.

"There's your money. Go and get it!"

Drunkenly, the gombeen-man lurched vaguely in the direction of the coins.

Laughing, Michael headed into the wood, with both horses. It would take hours for O'Callaghan, in his stupor, to find all the coins. With any luck, in his drunken state, he would fall asleep. When he woke up, he would have the problem of getting home, stark naked, without any clothes.

Reeking of whisky, who would believe any story that he told?

Chapter 20

Once he had helped her down from the tree, Elizabeth threw herself into his arms.

"Oh, Michael," she said, "I was so worried."

"Hush, *mavourneen*, I told you not to worry." He hugged her tight, weak with relief himself, then he carried her to where he had left the horses.

The mare whinnied when she saw Elizabeth.

"You brought Cloud," she said, smiling. "That mark on her head, it looks like a cloud."

Elizabeth rode Cloud, he took O'Callaghan's horse. Before they left, he threw the gun into the trees. Elizabeth laughed when he told her what he had done to the gombeen-man. Michael smiled to hide his worry. He knew that they only had a few hours, the night at best. The elation of outwitting O'Callaghan faded, to be replaced by a sense of foreboding. Whatever the gombeen-man said, by now Michael's absence from the village would be noted and suspicion would fall on him. Michael hoped and prayed that his family would not be blamed, but he was afraid that they would.

After a while, Elizabeth noticed his silence. She asked him what the matter was.

"I'm worried about my family," he said.

She understood that; she thought about it for a while. "What can they do that's worse than eviction?" she asked him. "They can't punish them for something you did."

"Eviction's bad enough," he said.

"Fraser said he was going to evict you anyway."

"When we get to America," he said, not voicing the fear that they never would, "the first thing we do is get the money to pay their fares over."

"Yes, of course," she said. Then, "Michael?"

"What?"

"I think," she said slowly, "that, once my father reads my letter, he'll call off the search."

"Why would he do that?"

"The scandal. There would be terrible gossip if it came out that Lord Roscawl's daughter had held up the factor and then run off with a boy from the village."

"They don't know I'm with you."

"They'll probably guess. But just think, Father O'Shaughnessy read my letter. He took the guns back to the castle. If they accuse anybody, he'll just say that he knows it was me."

"They were looking for you this morning, *mavourneen*."

"Yes, but that was before they knew that I held up Fraser. Once he thinks about it, my father will realize that it's best if I'm not caught. I think so, anyway."

Michael thought about what she had said. There was sense of a sort to it, he supposed.

They rode on toward the Comeragh mountains. Neither of them knew that, with the twin problems of Elizabeth's disappearance and the factor's robbery, Lord Roscawl had initially been too busy to see the priest and had told him to go away. Father O'Shaughnessy insisted though; he waited all day and finally, late in the evening, he was taken in to see the Lord.

In the early hours of the morning, they reached Cork. The city streets were quiet, many shops were boarded up. Michael had only been once to the city, many years ago with his father, but he remembered it as a busy, bustling place. After a while, they met a passer-by, who told them the way to O'Shea's Inn.

At the inn, he knocked on the door and waited. His Aunt Naimh opened it, peering at him for a time before she recognized him.

"Michael, is that you?"

"It is, Aunt Naimh."

"Come away in. What a surprise! It's good to see you, we were so worried about you."

"We've horses, Aunt Naimh."

"Well, take them round to the back. There's a place there to tether them."

Michael stood aside to let Elizabeth limp in.

"Who is this? It's not Liam, is it?"

He laughed. Elizabeth was still wearing the boy's clothes she had taken from the castle. "No," he said. "This is Elizabeth."

"What on earth?"

"I'll tell you later," he said, walking to the back yard, where he tied the reins of the horses to a post. He noticed that although there was a cart, the stable was empty. His aunt opened the back door and ushered him into the kitchen. Elizabeth was already seated by the fire. He sat down on a stool next to her. Soda bread was baking on a skillet over the fire; the smell made his mouth water. It had been a long time since he had eaten.

For the first time in more than twenty-four hours, Michael relaxed. Exhaustion swept over him in a wave; he had to struggle to keep his eyes from closing.

His uncle Conn came into the room. "Michael," he said, "I'm that glad to see you. Naimh and I've been worried."

Michael introduced Elizabeth, then slowly, he began to tell his story. When he was halfway through, his Aunt Naimh interrupted him with a plate of soda bread and salted herrings. He ate ravenously, so did Elizabeth. Then he finished telling them what had happened.

His aunt and uncle laughed when he told them that he had left the gombeen-man drunk and naked.

"What a tale," Conn said. "Michael, don't you worry about anything. I'll send your cousin Declan over to Roscawl, we'll bring them down here. It's not much, but at least it's a roof over their heads and they won't starve." He turned to Elizabeth. "You did the right thing, lass, trying to feed the village. I wish to God there was more like you."

Elizabeth smiled shyly.

Michael remembered his manners and asked Conn how they had been getting on themselves.

Conn shrugged, said they were managing. He used his mother's recipe to brew ale, and in the years before the potato blight it had been a good living – he had managed to buy the small inn that his family lived in now. Since the potato blight, though, trade had just about ground to a halt, nobody had any money any more. The worst thing was that he had to pay rates on the inn, and the rates were now twenty-five times what they had been before the blight, because of the need to raise money to pay for the Poor Law.

"I'll survive, though, because of the soldiers. I make a bob or two each week selling ale to the garrison."

Michael knew from his expression that he did not like taking money from the English army, but that he had no choice.

His cousin Declan came in, with his sisters. Naimh busied herself cooking their breakfast.

"Are there any boats in for America?" he asked Conn.

"There's always boats for America, these days. There'll be one leaving in the afternoon, at high tide."

Elizabeth cleared her throat. Shyly, she asked Conn if he would take care of her horse. She did not want to sell it to someone she did not know, and she trusted him.

"Of course I will, pet. I would pay you money for her, but I've none spare."

She smiled, relieved.

Michael stood up. "We'd best get going," he said. With Elizabeth's sore ankle, it would take a while to walk to the harbour at Cobh – the port that the English called Queenstown – and although he felt safe enough in his uncle's house, he would not feel really secure until he was on his way to America.

Naimh looked him up and down. "You're not going to America without a good pair of boots," she told him. "I've a pair of Conn's that'll do. And you could do with a clean shirt. Donal left one behind that you can have."

Once she had fitted Michael up with socks and boots, a

shirt and a sweater, she led Elizabeth into the other room, where she changed into the skirt and blouse that Michael's mother had given her. She gave Naimh the clothes she had been wearing, thinking that Declan could make use of them.

Naimh insisted on giving her a set of fresh underwear, a clean blouse and a heavy woollen cloak that would keep her warm on the journey.

Elizabeth was so touched that tears came to her eyes. These people were poor, she knew, yet they were willing, even eager to share what they had. The atmosphere in the tiny inn was happy, so different from the cold atmosphere of the castle. Naimh also gave them a couple of loaves of bread and some salted herrings.

Conn O'Shea went with them to Cobh. He knew some of the sailors, and he wanted to make sure they got a good boat. On the way, he told Michael to buy a sack of meal, because the rations on board ship were meagre and terrible.

Elizabeth was shocked at the poverty she saw in Cork. All the people were thin, and it seemed that most of them were beggars. It hurt her to have to ignore their pleas. The workhouse was full, Conn told her. A while ago, the managers had turned the women and children out, saying that there was room only for able-bodied men. It had taken a near riot to reverse the policy.

She wondered then what would become of Ireland – if the hunger would ever end.

A stage coach ran between Cork and Cobh; they decided to take it and pay the penny fare rather than risk missing the tide.

As they waited for the coach, Michael stopped by the hedgerow and gathered the wild flowers that grew there, dog roses and clovers, daisies and shamrock leaves. He hid the tiny bouquet under his jumper, ashamed that he had nothing else to give her.

At the harbour, Conn O'Shea looked around and then saw a boat he recognized. "Wait here," he told them.

Elizabeth shivered; the quayside was full of constables in uniform. Michael took her hand and squeezed it to reassure her. The constables were not looking for them, they were keeping a watch for smugglers.

Conn O'Shea came back with a tall, grizzled man who he introduced as Captain Ryan. Captain Ryan said there was space in his ship, as long as they did not mind sleeping in the crew's quarters. A deck hand had not turned up, so Michael could work his passage; he would only charge two guineas for Elizabeth, because they had their own food.

Michael wanted to give the money they had left to Conn for his mother, but Conn told him to keep it, because they might need it in America.

Conn hugged Michael and told him again not to worry about his family, then he hugged Elizabeth and wished her Godspeed.

A short while later, Elizabeth and Michael stood on deck, as the ship set sail for America.

"Remember when I told you that I wanted to go to America?" Michael asked her, putting his arm around her.

"Yes."

"Ach," he said, "it was daft, I thought. It was my wildest dream, that you and I would go to America. I never dared think that it might come true."

"That was my dream too," Elizabeth said.

His eyes met hers and then he kissed her briefly, shyly; as he pulled away he handed her the little bunch of wildflowers that he'd gathered for her.

Tears came to her eyes.

"I promise you," he said, "one day, I'll give you lilies and orchids."

She blinked. "You'll never be able to give me anything I love as much as these."

Historical Note

Before the potato crop began to fail in 1845, the plight of the Irish Catholic peasantry was precarious in the extreme. They tried to eke a living out of small patches of land, rented from Protestant landowners, paying the rent by selling the oats that they grew and living on the potatoes. When the potato crop failed, as it had done several times in the preceding thirty years, they faced starvation.

There was virtually no industry (apart from that around Belfast in the north) and hence no employment, with the exception perhaps of a few days' casual work during the harvest. A government inquiry in 1835 reported that three-quarters of the population were out of work.

The Westminster government was aware of the problems caused by crop failure and in late 1845 began to institute relief measures in the form of work schemes and kitchens that handed out food. The Corn Laws were repealed in 1846, allowing cheap Indian meal on to the market. Irish local government, in the form of the Poor Law Unions, managed by landowners and civic dignitaries, was encouraged to start similar schemes, to be paid for by locally levied rates.

In 1847, facing mounting costs, the government decided to end the national subsidy. Henceforth, relief schemes had to be funded entirely by rates. The result was disaster for Ireland; the food kitchens closed, work schemes were halted, and many of the Poor Law Unions were effectively bankrupted.

Meanwhile, people were dying. During the famine, one million people died, mainly in epidemics of diseases that flourish in people who do not have enough to eat. Another million emigrated; the population of Ireland has never recovered its pre-1845 levels.

The Westminster government was actually more concerned by the fear that Ireland would rebel. Revolution was rife in Europe in 1848; but in a country plagued by starvation there was neither the will nor the means to mount an armed insurrection. The efforts of the middle-class Young Irelanders to raise a rebel army were pathetic, and ended in a rout.

However Ireland, particularly Dublin, was flooded with troops. If the money spent on military measures had been diverted to famine relief, then the devastation, and bitterness, that ensued might have been avoided.

There were some charitable efforts, notably by the Quakers. A few landlords literally bankrupted themselves by buying food for their tenants or paying their fares to emigrate. Most landlords did the minimum required of them by law, all the while grumbling about the rising Poor Law rate.

The root of the Irish peasants' problem was land. The typical smallholding was not big enough to support a family, no more land was available to rent and as the population increased with succeeding generations the problem grew worse.

The Catholic Irish peasant had never forgotten or forgiven the English Protestant invasion, and the antipathy that existed between landlord and tenant was a result of that and also of the injustice inherent in the relationship between the impoverished majority and the wealthy minority.

During the famine, Ireland continued to export food – wheat and beef – to England. The failure of the Westminster government to take steps to ameliorate the predicament of the Irish people at that time made continuing unrest inevitable.

Look out for other new titles in the Forget Me Not series

Lavender Blue

Confused, not knowing what to do, Lily left and closed the door behind her, then collapsed on the landing, sobbing so loudly and heartbrokenly that she didn't hear the tramping of her father's boots as he came up the stairs.

"What-ho!" he called heartily. "Had a tiff, eh? Tell your old papa all about it."

Through her misery, Lily recognized that her father was sober for once. Perhaps it was too early for him to have got rollicking drunk, or maybe he had run out of money. He crouched down to Lily's level and put an arm around her, crooning, "There, there, then."

Lily rested her dark head against her father's ginger one. Nobody had inherited her father's colouring. Her brothers and sisters were all dark, apart from Archie, who still hadn't sprouted a single hair.

"I was only doing my best," Lily gasped through her sobs. "I thought it would help!" She raised huge, drowned grey eyes up to her father's green ones.

Her father rearranged himself into a more comfortable sitting position and pulled Lily onto his lap as if she had been a toddler. "Now, kindly start this story from the beginning so that I can understand," he ordered gently.

"Well, you know how much I like singing? And you know I lost my job at Collyers? I know this boy called Billy who sings outside the Old Mo…"

Lily unfolded her story.

"And Mother thought I had earned the money by working as a … a…" She knew the bad word, "prostitute", but couldn't say it.

"I think I know what you mean." Her father stood up and pulled her to her feet. "We all think you have a very sweet voice, Lily, but singing, that sort of singing especially, is no way for a young lady to earn a living. I understand how you wanted to help us out – it's very generous of you, m'dear, and no more than I would expect from a child of mine, but really, this singing lark has got to end or it'll be the death of your mother. Promise me that you'll never go out singing again!"

Lily gazed at her father and bit her lip. She nodded half-heartily and mumbled, "I promise."

"Louder…" he insisted.

"*I promise!*"

"That's better. Now, let's go in and explain all this to your mother…"

Lily had to repeat the same promise to her mother no fewer than five times before she was satisfied. Then Harry came in and when he heard about the goings-on, he grinned wickedly. "Well, you can't say I spilled the beans, Sis, though I have to admit now that I did know about it. You see, I've seen you." He looked utterly triumphant.

"You never!" Lily gasped. "Where?"

"Outside the Oxford, when I took Dora to a show."

"Oho? So the market are paying you enough to take

young ladies out, are they? When I was your age…"

Lily had no wish to hear her father's reminiscence. This was talk between men. She excused herself and went into the other room, where she splashed cold water over her face from the bowl on the dressing-table and tried to repair the ravages of her crying fit.

She was sitting on the edge of the bed, attempting to read a book by candlelight, when her mother tapped on the door and came in.

"Did you mean it about the blouse?" she said.

Lily gave her a watery smile.

"Thank you, dear, I'll treasure it, but you must have the rest of the money back."

"Nonsense! Put it towards food for us all," insisted Lily.

Her mother hesitated, then took a step towards her and enfolded Lily in her arms. "I'm sorry I was so angry, dear. You know my bad temper!" she apologized. "I do fly off the handle. These headaches don't help…"

"It's all right," said Lily. Her mother seemed in the right mood for her to bring up the burning subject, so she tried. "Mother," she began, "you know we could do with more money and I could earn more than Harry and Father put together if you would only let me go out singing."

"*No!*" Her mother was utterly emphatic. "Never!" she added for emphasis. "I would far rather starve than have you cheapen yourself in that way, acting like a gypsy or a beggarwoman. No, your father and Harry and I will all do our best to find you something. Besides, now that I am getting that big order that Mrs Booth-Edwards mentioned in her letter, I shall need you to help me. If you can learn to do some of the sewing, you will be earning your keep."

"Oh, Mother! You know I can't sew!" Lily protested.

"I think that, with a little effort and concentration…" Lily's concentration left her and she let her mother ramble on, conscious only of the leaden weight in her heart. She couldn't sing… She wasn't to be allowed to experience ever again that wonderful, soaring feeling of having power over an audience… Never again would she hear the applause, hear the chink of coins being thrown her way. *And she wouldn't see Billy!* That was the worst thought of all.

Thanks to Lily's nest-egg, Christmas 1898 was the best Christmas they had ever had. On Christmas Day there was a big stuffed turkey, potatoes and sprouts and plum pudding to follow. Mr Cobbett had begged, borrowed or stolen a bottle of brandy and they all got a bit merry. In fact, it seemed the brandy even penetrated through his mother's milk to Archie, because he was extremely gurgly and good-tempered and slept like a log for two nights running.

On Boxing Day, Millie brought her family to visit. She and her husband Gerald had two-year-old twin girls. The day after that, they went to visit Edie and George. Lily really missed Elizabeth, who had written to say that she was needed by her employers and couldn't get away.

Once the excitement of Christmas and New Year were over, Lily started to fret. The weather was terribly cold – snow winds all the way from Siberia, everybody said. When Lily took the jug down to the milk cart, the milk-man had to chip the milk from his churn and drop it into the jug in frozen chunks. It was said that a cab horse's hooves had frozen to the road and it could only be released after considerable efforts with a burning brand, which set fire to the unfortunate animal's fetlocks.

The Cobbett family were suffering, too. There was little work at the market as much of the produce could not get through since the main routes were blocked by snowfalls. Harry and Father spent more time than usual at the inn and as for Lily, the strain of not seeing Billy, and not being able to sing, made her feel as dull and despondent as a prisoner in a cell.

Then, three weeks into January, her mother's ever-present cough suddenly grew considerably worse and she took to her bed, leaving Lily to look after Archie. Although she took the baby to her mother at feeding times, it seemed the milk she was providing was deficient, because the baby was thin and sickly-looking and, like his mother, grew worse every day.

Father and Harry, spending little time at home, seemed oblivious to the extent of the tragedy unfolding beneath their own roof.

"Oh, it's just a little winter cold," Father said cheerfully, while Mother, not wishing to worry him, nodded her agreement. But Lily could see that it was something far, far worse and one day, when her mother appeared flushed and listless and thrust Archie away from her, she realized that something just had to be done.

She took the fretful baby down to Mrs Molloy, saying, "Please could you look after him? Just for an hour? I must go out on some errands and Mother isn't well."

The fat, motherly woman frowned. "I've heard that cough of hers. Terrible, it is. Tell you what, I'll mix her up some of my potion. You can take it up to her when you come back."

Lily thanked her and made her escape, leaving Mrs Molloy rocking Archie to and fro in her arms in front of a fire that was far hotter than the flickering, spitting one in the grate upstairs.

It was matinée time. Lily would be lucky to find a queue which didn't already have its busker. But she was lucky. The Drury Lane Theatre itself had a queue just begging to be entertained, and Lily set about entertaining it.

That day she happened to be wearing her blue coat with a purplish blue shawl thrown over it, one of her mother's which she had "borrowed". She hadn't worn the coat for some time as it wasn't her warmest, but the colour had appealed to her today and she thought she was unlikely to freeze to death in half an hour. Halfway through a song, she thrust her icy hands into her pockets and the fingertips of her left hand encountered something bristly. When she took it out, she found it to be a sprig of lavender, the stalks bound in blue cotton. She remembered now. She had last worn the coat when visiting her sister Edie. Edie had been making lavender bags and had given Lily some sprigs she had left over. She thought she had put them all in with the bedding, to sweeten and freshen it, but this one had somehow got left behind in her pocket.

She sniffed it, then suddenly the words of an old song came to her. *Lavender Blue...* She sang it, and on an impulse she changed the words to, "When you are king, diddle, diddle, I shall be queen." She smiled as she sang, and she kept the sprig of lavender clasped in her fingers, sniffing it from time to time. It made her think of summer in warmer, sweeter, far-off climes where nobody ever died of cold in winter.

"While you and I, diddle, diddle, keep ourselves warm…"

She didn't realize how much longing she put into those words, or how the expression on her face affected her audience, but several tears were wiped away and the applause was long and the coins generous in amount.

The crowd started filtering into the theatre. Lily gathered up her money, hoping it would be enough to pay for a doctor and for the vital medicine she felt sure both her mother and baby Archie needed. She stood up, about to go, when a man came walking up to her.

"That voice," he said. "I've missed it. I used to hear it coming from a window in Betterton Street but I haven't heard it for a long time. I thought you must have gone away."

Lily gave him a quizzical look. He was well-dressed and in early middle-age, and there was something about him that was ever so slightly familiar.

"My mother is ill, so we have had to keep quiet at home," she explained.

"I'm sorry to hear that." He withdrew a card from a leather folder in the inside pocket of his thick velour overcoat. Lily placed it in her own pocket without looking at it, as it seemed ill-mannered to do so while he was still standing there.

"Have you ever worked inside a theatre, as opposed to outside?" he asked her.

Lily shook her head.

"I think that you could go far with that voice," he said. "What is your name, child?"

"Lily Cobbett," she replied.

"Hmm. We'll have to think of a more attractive name for you than that. Lily is all right, but *Cobbett*…" He took a step back and narrowed his eyes thoughtfully. "Lavender Blue," he said. "How about that? You could wear a pretty lavender dress and that song could be one you open your act with. Not end it, mind – don't want to leave 'em crying. Start them off with a sob in their hearts, then cheer them up with something happy. What do you think?"

Lily had no idea what he was talking about.

"Come and see me one morning, around eleven," he said. "Ask for me at the main door. Don't forget, will you?"

Lily stared at him and nodded, then shook her head. She felt completely confused. Who was he to tell her that there was something wrong with her name and she should change it to Lavender Blue?

He fished in his pocket, withdrew a coin and pressed it into her hand. Then he disappeared into the theatre. Lily noticed how the doormen touched the peaks of their caps as he passed them. He was obviously a man of some importance.

However, she was robbed of a chance to glance at his card by the sudden appearance of a tiny, bearded hunchback.

"Hello, Titch," she greeted him.

"Jago was wondering what happened to you," he said.

She told him about being banned from performing, and handed over the regulation share of the money, completely forgetting about the gentleman's coin, which was sitting next to his card in her pocket.

"If you're starting again, you must come and see Jago or else he will be angry," Titch said warningly.

"That won't be necessary," chimed in another voice and a tall male figure stepped out of the shadows.

"Billy!" cried Lily in delight. "Oh Billy, it's so good to see you. I—"

The eager smile was dashed from her face by the cold look in his eyes. His icicle stare swept her from head to foot, chilling her even more than the east wind that was blowing. Titch, sensing that something private and personal was going on, scuttled off towards the next theatre, while tears sprang to Lily's eyes. Oh, she had missed him so much! Why was he acting this way? Did he think she had been avoiding him deliberately?

"I haven't been allowed out," she explained. "Now Mother and the baby are very sick so I need money for the doctor."

"And you never thought of coming to find me? I could have helped you, Lily. You could have sung with me. But from what I've just overheard, this isn't the first time you've busked on your own."

Lily hung her head. "No," she admitted. "I was hoping you wouldn't find out."

"I never thought we'd end up as…" He hesitated for an instant, then said, "*rivals*," very emphatically.

"But we're not! There are plenty of theatres, there's room for both of us to sing," she pointed out.

"We both do the same sort of material," he said. "And you have the advantage of being a pretty girl."

Normally, being called "pretty" by Billy would have made her glow with pleasure, but the way he had just said it made it sound more like an insult.

Still, she wasn't going to let him win this argument. "What about the songs you write? Nobody else sings those," she said. Then, in an effort to mend things between them, she said, "And I meant it about teaching you to read and write. As soon as the weather and Mother's health improve…"

Billy gave a disbelieving toss of his head. "You never intended wasting your time on someone like me! You were just awaiting your opportunity to get spotted by the likes of James Graydon. You *used* me, Lily!"

Lily hardly heard his last accusation. "Who's James Graydon?" she asked him.

"The man who gave you his card. I saw everything. That's what I meant when I said it wouldn't be necessary for you to have anything to do with Jago any more."

"I really have no idea what you're talking about," Lily said, utterly perplexed.

"James Graydon is the manager of the Old Mo, Lily. And, from the way he was talking, he obviously intends to put you on the stage and turn you into a music-hall star!"

The
White Cockade

Ewan roused himself. "You're afraid of blood poisoning," he said, baldly. "Don't think I haven't thought of it, too."

"It's been three days," she had to say.

"Aye – but, I've bled enough to wash out anything…" He turned his head away weakly and she urged him to drink more.

"Give it to Sandy, he must be starved."

"Na, na, I've had my fill o' oatcakes," the boy said stoutly. "You drink up, now. It's good it'll be after doing you."

Ewan obeyed but after a few sips fell asleep like a tired child.

"He's no well," Sandy commented.

"No," Jenna agreed with a sigh. "He needs a doctor. I don't know what should be done for him."

"Where's Himself? He'd ken fine."

Jenna had forgotten her grandfather. "He went to Inverness to look for Ewan –"

As if disturbed by his name, the man at their feet moaned and stirred restlessly. Jenna bent to tuck the blankets closer.

"I'd better go up – the soldiers are due back any time," she said. "I'll be down again as soon as I can."

But that promise proved much more difficult than she

had supposed. The soldiers returned shortly before dusk. Quickly, they ensconced themselves in the outbuildings, cooking their evening meal over fires they lit in the courtyard. James Farnby, having joined her for dinner, showed every sign of intending to spend the rest of the evening in her company. For a while their conversation ranged over various matters; they even discovered mutual acquaintances in London. Then, suddenly, when she was lulled into almost forgetting that he was a military man in Scotland to quell a rebellion, he asked casually, out of nowhere, where the Prince's gold was hidden.

Eyes wide, she stared at him blankly. "What gold?" she demanded. "Why should I know where it is?"

He studied her closely. "Rumour has it, that it is hidden in this area, in a cave."

Her heart fluttered at the word, but she did her best to hide the sudden suspicion that struck her. To her relief the lieutenant appeared to be unaware of the agitation he had caused and was still speaking evenly.

"We know a large amount was landed on the west coast from a French ship," he went on. "Obviously, as the Stuart Pretender's headquarters were in Inverness, it would have been brought in this direction."

"This is the first I've heard of it," Jenna told him truthfully. Almost wistfully, she had a fleeting memory of her former life, when the only gold she had heard of was her mother's housekeeping money and rebellion was something only to be read about in newspapers.

Grey eyes searched her face and she forced herself to meet his gaze steadily. At last his manner relaxed as if satisfied and he smiled into her anxious face.

"I believe you," he assured her. "These are dangerous times, Miss Marsden. I would be your friend. Promise me that—" He broke off suddenly.

"What were you going to ask me?" she enquired when it had become clear that he was not about to continue.

He looked at her. "I have no right… But I was going to ask you to trust me. I would be happy to give you my protection – while your grandfather is absent, of course. If you could forget that we seem to be on opposite sides of this wretched affair."

Jenna caught her breath as their eyes held. She realized, with a leap of pleasure, that the attraction she had felt from the first, for the tall fellow countryman was mutual.

"I should be very happy if we could be friends," she returned, quietly, "Grandfather is for the king, I believe many in the Highlands are loyal … and so, of course, am I."

"Good. Then, we can have no argument."

"No," she agreed, hoping any lingering doubt she felt was absent from her voice and manner. Mindful of the men in the cellar, she knew that she was being economical with the truth. If James Farnby discovered Ewan and Sandy, his reaction would be more than merely an "argument", she thought uneasily.

Jenna had hoped to pay a visit to the cellar before going to bed, but Lieutenant Farnby showed no sign of retiring before her. At last there was nothing for it but to go to her room, where Mairi was already asleep, before her excuses aroused his suspicions. Wrapping herself in her plaid, she sat by the window listening for the Redcoat to come upstairs. At last she heard his footsteps on the stairs and watched the glow from his candle show briefly under her door as he passed on his way to his room.

Waiting impatiently, until she judged he was in bed and asleep, she crept across the floor and opened the door. A shaft of moonlight shone through the narrow window like a knife-blade, doing little more than illuminate the floor-boards where it fell, leaving the rest of the landing in inky darkness. All was quiet and, after a moment, she slipped carefully to the head of the staircase.

She had reached the hall below and was feeling her way towards the kitchen, when she became convinced that she was not the only one moving cautiously around Duntore. An icy shiver trickled down her spine as the hair on the back of her neck rose in primeval fear.

A faint thud as someone stumbled, accompanied by a muffled curse, came from nearby. Relieved that her fellow nocturnal explorer was human and not some ghostly former inhabitant, Jenna gathered her wits, realizing the need for some excuse.

Humming under her breath, in what she hoped was a care-free manner, she continued towards the kitchen. Discarding her former caution, she opened the door, letting the latch rattle. Reaching the fireplace, she poked a taper into the banked-down peats and stretched up to light the candle on the shelf above. As light flooded the room, she turned and saw a figure in the doorway.

Not needing to pretend her fright, she jumped and gave a startled cry, loud enough, she hoped to warn the men in the cellar. Dropping the taper, which flared briefly and went out, she stared at the silent man. As he came forward, she saw that the lieutenant had discarded his red coat and looked much more human in white shirt and breeches. She was interested to see that his hair, which was brushed free of powder, was a warm brown.

"Y-you frightened me!" she accused, breathlessly.

"My apologies." He advanced into the room, eyeing her enquiringly. "May one ask why you are wandering around at this time of night?"

She raised her own eyebrows in imitation. "I would ask you the same question," she returned, thinking that attack was the best defence. "And, I sir, I would remind you, live here and so can really do what I please!"

He smiled pleasantly, showing even teeth. "True," he agreed, "but I was aroused by sounds of movement. What is your excuse?"

"I do not need one. If you must know, I needed a drink."

He allowed his gaze to travel over her. "It's past midnight and you are fully dressed," he pointed out. "If I were a suspicious man, I would think you had been waiting until you thought me asleep."

"Why should I do that?" Jenna asked lightly, pouring milk from a jug and making a show of toasting him, before drinking it. "Allow me a little sense. You appear a civil, honourable gentleman, but soldiers have a name for certain behaviour – and, I am an unprotected female. Under the circumstances, it would be foolish, you must agree, to wander around the house in a state of undress."

He nodded gravely, his eyes twinkling. "You are very wise – under the circumstances," he agreed, with a teasing look, that made her heart flutter.

His shirt was open at the neck and she could see a pulse beating in his bare throat. Without his stiff uniform, he seemed much more friendly, his manner less formal. Suddenly, he stepped forward and to her surprise, took her hand.

Carrying it to his lips, he astonished her by kissing the back of her fingers. "We have not met in the most auspicious of circumstances," he began, holding her eyes with his, "but I would like you to think well of me... It would give me great pleasure if we could be friends."

Jenna could only stare at him, wondering if her cousin could hear and, taking her silence for surprise, he hurried on: "Do not think me impertinent, but fortune has brought us together and we military men are taught to seize the opportunity when it arises!" He looked at her a shade anxiously. "You are not angry?"

She shook her head. "No. Somewhat surprised."

He had retained his grip on her hand and now he pulled her gently towards him. Before she realized what was his intention, he had tilted her head and kissed her. Taken unawares, her lips opened slightly under his mouth. Knowing that a well brought up young lady would instantly demand to be unhanded, she was mortified to find herself melting into his embrace.